THE ROYAL GAME

THE WORKS OF STEFAN ZWEIG

Fiction

BEWARE OF PITY
CONFLICTS
KALEIDOSCOPE
THE BURIED CANDELABRUM

Memoirs

THE WORLD OF YESTERDAY: An Autobiography

Biographies

CONQUEROR OF THE SEAS: The Story of Magellan
THE RIGHT TO HERESY: Castellio Against Calvin
MARY, QUEEN OF SCOTLAND AND THE ISLES
ERASMUS OF ROTTERDAM
MARIE ANTOINETTE: The Portrait of an Average Woman
JOSEPH FOUCHÉ: The Portrait of a Politician
MENTAL HEALERS: Mesmer · Mary Baker Eddy · Freud
AMERIGO: A Comedy of Errors in History

Plays

JEREMIAH
VOLPONE

History

BRAZIL: Land of the Future
THE TIDE OF FORTUNE: Twelve Historical Miniatures

Belles Lettres

MASTER BUILDERS

BY STEFAN ZWEIG

THE ROYAL GAME

AMOK

LETTER FROM
AN UNKNOWN WOMAN

NEW YORK

THE VIKING PRESS

1946

COPYRIGHT 1944 BY THE VIKING PRESS, INC.

THE ROYAL GAME, TRANSLATED BY B. W. HUEBSCH
AMOK (COPYRIGHT 1931) AND LETTER FROM AN
UNKNOWN WOMAN (COPYRIGHT 1932) TRANSLATED
BY EDEN AND CEDAR PAUL

PRINTED IN U. S. A. BY THE VAIL-BALLOU PRESS, INC.

PUBLISHED BY THE VIKING PRESS
IN APRIL 1944

SECOND PRINTING, MARCH, 1946

⤐⤐⤐ ⸱ ⸱⸱⸱

PUBLISHED ON THE SAME DAY IN THE DOMINION OF
CANADA BY THE MACMILLAN COMPANY OF CANADA
LIMITED

CONTENTS

THE ROYAL GAME

The big liner, due to sail from New York to Buenos Aires at midnight, was filled with the activity and bustle incident to the last hour. Visitors who had come to see their friends off pressed hither and thither, page-boys with caps smartly cocked slithered through the public rooms shouting names snappily, baggage, parcels and flowers were being hauled about, inquisitive children ran up and down companion-ways, while the deck orchestra provided persistent accompaniment. I stood talking to an acquaintance on the promenade deck somewhat apart from the hubbub when two or three flash-lights sprayed sharply near us, evidently for press photos of some prominent passenger at a last-minute interview. My friend looked in that direction and smiled.

"You have a queer bird on board, that Czentovic."

And as my face must have revealed that the statement meant nothing to me he added, by way of explanation, "Mirko Czentovic, the world chess champion. He has just finished off the U.S.A. in a coast-to-coast exhibition tour and is on his way to capture Argentina."

This served to recall not only the name of the young world champion but, too, a few details relating to his rocket-like career; my friend, a more observant newspaper reader than I, was able to eke them out with a string of anecdotes. At a single stroke, about a year ago, Czentovic had aligned himself with the solidest Elder

Statesmen of the art of chess, such as Alekhin, Capablanca, Tartakover, Lasker, Boguljubov; not since the appearance of the nine-year-old prodigy, Reshevsky, in New York in 1922 had a newcomer crashed into the famed guild to the accompaniment of such widespread interest. It seems that Czentovic's intellectual equipment, at the beginning, gave small promise of so brilliant a career. The secret soon seeped through that in his private capacity this champion wasn't able to write a single sentence in any language without misspelling a word, and that, as one of his vexed colleagues, wrathfully sarcastic, put it, "He enjoys equal ignorance in every field of culture." His father, a poverty-stricken Yugoslavian boatman on the Danube, had been run down in his tiny vessel one night by a grain steamer, and the orphaned boy, then twelve, was taken in charge by the pastor of their obscure village out of pity. The good man did his level best to instil into the indolent, slow-speaking, low-browed child at home what he seemed unable to grasp in the village school.

But all efforts proved vain. Mirko stared blankly at the writing exercise just as if the strokes had not already been explained a hundred times; his lumbering brain lacked every power to grasp even the simplest subjects. At fourteen he still added with his fingers, and it was only by dint of great strain that he read in a book or newspaper. Yet none could say that Mirko was unwilling or disobedient. Whatever he was told to do he did: fetched water, split wood, worked in the field, washed up the kitchen, and he could be relied upon to execute— even if with exasperating slowness—every service that was demanded. But what grieved the kindly pastor most about the blockhead was his total lack of co-operation.

He performed no deed unless specially directed, asked no questions, never played with other lads, and sought no occupation of his own accord; after Mirko had concluded his work about the house, he would sit idly with that empty stare of grazing sheep without participating in the slightest in what might be going on. Evenings, while the pastor sucked at his long peasant pipe and played his customary three games of chess with the police-sergeant, the fair-haired dull-wit squatted silent alongside them and stared from under his heavy lids, seemingly sleepy and indifferent, at the checkered board.

One winter evening, while the two men were absorbed in their daily game, a rapid crescendo of bells gave notice of a quickly approaching sleigh. A peasant, his cap covered with snow, stomped in hastily to tell the pastor that his mother lay dying and to ask his immediate attendance in the hope that there was still time to administer extreme unction. The priest accompanied him instanter. The police-sergeant, who had not yet finished his beer, lighted a fresh pipe preparatory to leaving and was about to draw on his heavy sheepskin boots when he noticed how immovably Mirko's gaze was fastened on the board with its interrupted game.

"Well, do you want to finish it?" he said jocularly, fully convinced that the sleepyhead had no notion of how to move a single piece. The boy looked up shyly, nodded assent, and took the pastor's place. After fourteen moves the sergeant was beaten and he had to concede that his defeat was in no wise attributable to avoidable carelessness. The second game resulted similarly.

"Balaam's ass!" cried the astounded pastor upon his return, explaining to the policeman, a lesser expert in the Bible, that two thousand years ago there had been a like miracle of a dumb being suddenly endowed with the speech of wisdom. The late hour notwithstanding, the goodly pater could not forgo challenging his half-illiterate helper to a contest. Mirko won from him, too, with ease. He played toughly, slowly, deliberately, never once raising his bowed broad brow from the board. But he played with irrefutable certainty and in the days that followed neither the priest nor the policeman was able to win a single game.

The priest, best able to assess his ward's various short-comings, now became curious as to the manner in which this one-sided singular gift would resist a severer test. After Mirko had been made somewhat presentable by the efforts of the village barber, he drove him in his sleigh to the near-by small town where he knew that many chess players—a cut above him in ability, he was aware from experience—were always present in the café on the main square. The pastor's entrance, as he steered the straw-haired, red-cheeked fifteen-year-old before him, created no small stir in the circle; the boy, in his sheep-fell (woolen side in) and high boots, eyes shyly downcast, stood aside until summoned to a chess-table. Mirko lost in the first encounter because his master had never em-ployed the Sicilian defence. The next game, with the best player of the lot, resulted in a draw. But in the third and fourth and all that came after he slew them, one after the other.

It so happens that little provincial towns of Yugoslavia are seldom the theatre of exciting events; consequently, this first appearance of the peasant champion before the assembled worthies became no less than a sensation. It was unanimously decided to keep the boy in town until the next day for a special gathering of the chess club and, in particular, for the benefit of Count Simczic of the castle, a chess fanatic. The priest, who now regarded his ward with quite a new pride, but whose joy of discovery was subordinate to the sense of duty which called him home to his Sunday service, consented to leave him for further tests. The chess group put young Czentovic up at the local hotel where he saw a water-closet for the first time in his life.

The chess room was crowded to capacity Sunday afternoon. Mirko faced the board immobile for four hours, spoke no word, and never looked up; one player after another fell before him. Finally a multiple game was proposed; it took a while before they could make clear to the novice that he had to play against several contestants at one and the same time. No sooner had Mirko grasped the procedure than he adapted himself to it, and he trod slowly with heavy, creaking shoes from table to table, eventually winning seven of the eight games.

Grave consultations now took place. True, strictly speaking, the new champion was not of the town, yet the innate national pride had received a lively fillip. Here was a chance, at last, for this town, so small that its existence was hardly suspected, to put itself on the map by sending a great man into the world. A vaudeville agent named Koller, who supplied the local garrison cabaret with talent, offered to obtain professional training for the youth from a Viennese expert whom he knew and to see him through for a year if the deficit were made good. Count Simczic, who in his sixty years of daily chess had never encountered so remarkable an antagonist, signed the guaranty promptly. That day marked the opening of the astonishing career of the Danube boatman's son.

It took only six months for Mirko to master every secret of chess technique, though with one odd limitation which later became apparent to the game's votaries and caused a sneer. Czentovic never was able to memorize a single game or, to use the professional term, to play blind. He lacked completely the ability to conceive the board in the limitless space of the imagination. He had to have the field of sixty-four black and white squares and the thirty-two pieces tangibly before him; even when he had attained international fame he carried a folding pocket board with him in order to be able to reconstruct a game or work on a problem by visual means. This defect, in itself not important, betrayed a want of imaginative power and provoked animated discussions among chess fans similar to those in musical circles when it proves that an outstanding virtuoso or conductor is unable to play or direct without a score. This singularity, however, was no obstacle to Mirko's stupendous rise. At seventeen he already possessed a dozen prizes, at eighteen he won the Hungarian mastery, and finally, at twenty, the championship of the world. The boldest experts, every one of them immeasurably his superior in brains, imagination, and audacity, fell before his tough, cold logic as did Napoleon before the clumsy Kutusov and Hannibal before Fabius Cunctator, of whom Livy records that his traits of phlegm and imbecility were already conspicuous in his childhood. Thus it occurred that the illustrious gallery of chess masters, which included eminent representatives of widely varied intellectual fields —philosophers, mathematicians, constructive, imaginative, and often creative talents—was invaded by a complete outsider, a heavy, taciturn peasant clod from whom not even the cunningest journalists were ever able to extract a word that would help to make a story. Yet, however he may have deprived the newspapers of polished phrases, substitutes in the way of anecdotes about his person were numerous, for, inescapably, the moment he arose from the board at which he was the incomparable master, Czentovic became a grotesque, an almost comic figure. In spite of his correct dress, his fashionable cravat with its too ostentatious pearl stickpin, and his carefully manicured nails, he remained in manners and behaviour the narrow-minded lout who swept the priest's kitchen. He utilized his gift and his fame to squeeze out all the money they would yield, displaying petty and often vulgar greed, always with a shameless clumsiness that aroused his professional colleagues' ridicule and anger. He travelled from town to town, stopped at the cheapest hotels, played for any club that would pay his fee, sold the advertising rights in his portrait to a soap manufacturer, and oblivious of his competitors' scorn—they being aware that he hardly knew how to write—attached his name to a "Philosophy of Chess" that had been written by a hungry Galician student for a business-minded publisher. As with all leathery dispositions, he was wanting in any appreciation of the ludicrous; from the time he became champion he regarded himself as the most important man in the world, and the consciousness of having beaten all of those clever, intellectual, brilliant speakers and writers in their own field and of earning more than they, transformed his early unsureness into a cold and awkwardly flaunted pride.

"And how can one expect that such rapid fame should fail to befuddle so empty a head?" concluded my friend who had just advanced those classic examples of Czentovic's childish lust for rank. "Why shouldn't a twenty-one-year-old lad from the Banat be afflicted with a frenzy of vanity if, suddenly, by merely shoving figures around on a wooden board, he can earn more in a week than his whole village does in a year by chopping down trees under the bitterest conditions? Besides, isn't it damned easy to take yourself for a great man if you're not burdened with the slightest suspicion that a Rembrandt, a Beethoven, a Dante, a Napoleon, ever even existed? There's just one thing in that immured brain of his—the knowledge that he hasn't lost a game of chess for months, and as he happens not to dream that the world holds other values than chess and money, he has every ground to be infatuated with himself."

The information communicated by my friend could not fail to excite my special curiosity. I have always been fascinated by all types of monomania, by persons wrapped up in a single idea; for the stricter the limits a man sets for himself, the more clearly he approaches the eternal. Just such seemingly world-aloof persons create their own remarkable and quite unique world-in-little, and work, termite-like, in their particular medium. Thus I made no bones about my intention to examine this specimen of one-track intellect under a magnifying glass during the twelve-day journey to Rio.

"You'll be out of luck," my friend warned me. "As far as I know, nobody has succeeded in extracting the least bit of psychological material from Czentovic. Underneath all his abysmal limitations this sly farmhand conceals the wisdom not to expose himself; the procedure is simple: except for such compatriots of his own sphere as he contrives to meet in ordinary taverns he avoids all conversation. When he senses a person of culture he retreats into his shell; that's why nobody can plume himself on having heard him say something stupid or on having sounded the presumably bottomless depths of his ignorance."

As a matter of fact, my friend was right. It proved utterly impossible to approach Czentovic during the first few days of the voyage, unless by rude intrusion, which, of course, isn't my way. He did, sometimes, appear on the promenade deck, but then always with hands clasped behind his back in a posture of dignified self-absorption, like Napoleon in the familiar painting; and, at that, those peripatetic exhibitions were told off in such haste and so jerkily that to gain one's end one would have had to trot after him. The social halls, the bar, the smoking-room, saw nothing of him. A steward of whom I made confidential inquiries revealed that he spent the greater part of the day in his cabin with a large chess-board on which he recapitulated games or worked out new problems.

After three days it angered me to think that his defence tactics were more effective than my will to approach him. I had never before had a chance to know a great chess player personally, and the more I now sought to familiarize myself with the type, the more incomprehensible seemed a lifelong brain activity that rotated exclusively about a space composed of sixty-four black and white squares. I was well aware from my own experience of the mysterious attraction of the royal game, this one among all games contrived by man which rises superior to the tyranny of chance and which bestows its palms only on mental attainment, or rather on a definite form of mental endowment. But is it not an offensively narrow construction to call chess a game? Is it not a science too, a technique, an art, that sways among these categories as Mahomet's coffin does between heaven and earth, at once a union of all contradictory concepts: primeval yet ever new; mechanical in operation yet effective only through the imagination; bounded in geometric space though boundless in its combinations; ever-developing yet sterile; thought that leads to nothing; mathematics that produces no result; art without works; architecture without substance, and nevertheless, as proved by evidence, more lasting in its being and presence than all books and achievements; the only game that belongs to all peoples and all ages and of which none knows the divinity that bestowed it on the world to slay boredom, to sharpen the senses, to exhilarate the spirit. One searches for its beginning and for its end. Children can learn its simple rules, duffers succumb to its temptation, yet within this immutable tight square it creates a particular species of master not to be compared with any other—persons destined for chess alone, specific geniuses in whom vision, patience, and technique are operative through a distribution no less precisely ordained than in mathematicians, poets, composers, but merely united on a different level. In the heyday of physiognomical research a Gall would perhaps have dissected the brains of such masters of chess to establish whether a particular coil in the grey matter of the brain, a sort of chess muscle or chess bump, was more conspicuously developed than in other skulls. How a physiognomist would have been fascinated by the case of a Czentovic where that which is genius appears interstratified with an absolute inertia of the intellect like a single vein of gold in a ton of dead rock! It stands to reason that so unusual a game, one touched with genius, must create out of itself fitting matadors. This I always knew, but what was difficult and almost impossible to conceive of was the life of a mentally alert person whose

world contracts to a narrow, black-and-white one-way
street; who seeks ultimate triumphs in the to-and-fro,
forward and backward movement of thirty-two pieces; a
being who, by a new opening in which the knight is
preferred to the pawn, apprehends greatness and the
immortality that goes with casual mention in a chess
handbook—of a man of spirit who, escaping madness,
can unremittingly devote all of his mental energy during
ten, twenty, thirty, forty years to the ludicrous effort to
corner a wooden king on a wooden board!

And here, for the first time, one of these phenomena,
one of these singular geniuses (or shall I say puzzling
fools?) was close to me, six cabins distant, and I, unfor-
tunate, for whom curiosity about mental problems manifested itself in a kind of passion, seemed unable to effect
my purpose. I conjured up the absurdest ruses: tickle his
vanity by the offer of an interview in an important paper, or engage his greed by proposing a lucrative exhibition tour of Scotland. Finally it occurred to me that the
hunter's never-failing practice is to lure the woodcock by
imitating its mating cry, so what more successful way was
there of attracting a chess master's attention to oneself
than by playing chess?

At no time had I ever permitted chess to absorb me
seriously, for the simple reason that it meant nothing to
me but a pastime; if I spend an hour at the board it is not
because I want to subject myself to a strain but, on the
contrary, to relieve mental tension. I "play" at chess in
the literal sense of the word whereas to real devotees it is
serious business. Chess, like love, cannot be played alone,
and up to that time I had no idea whether there were
other chess lovers on board. In order to attract them from
their lairs I set a primitive trap in the smoking-room in

that my wife (whose game is even weaker than mine) and I sat at a chess-board as a decoy. Surely enough, we had made no more than six moves when one passerby stopped, another asked permission to watch, and before long the desired partner materialized. MacIver was his name; a Scottish foundation-engineer who, I learned, had made a large fortune boring for oil in California. He was a robust specimen with an almost square jaw and strong teeth, and a rich complexion pronouncedly rubicund as a result, at least in part surely, of copious indulgence in whiskey. His conspicuously broad, almost vehemently athletic shoulders made themselves unpleasantly notice-able in his game, for this MacIver typified those self-important worshippers of success who regard defeat in even a harmless contest as a blow to their self-esteem. Accustomed to achieving his ends ruthlessly and spoiled by material success, this massive self-made man was so thoroughly saturated with his sense of superiority that opposition of any kind became undue resistance if not insult. After losing the first round he sulked and began to explain in detail, and dictatorially, that it would not have happened but for a momentary oversight; in the third he ascribed his failure to the noise in the adjoin-ing room; never would he lose a game without at once demanding revenge. This ambitious crabbedness amused me at first but as time went on I accepted it as the un-avoidable accompaniment to my real purpose—to tempt the world master to our table.

By the third day it worked—but only half-way. It may be that Czentovic observed us at the chess-board through a window from the promenade deck or that he just hap-pened to be honouring the smoking-room with his pres-ence; anyway, as soon as he perceived us interlopers toy-

ing with the tools of his trade, he involuntarily stepped
a little nearer and, keeping a deliberate distance, cast a
searching glance at our board. It was MacIver's move.
This one move was sufficient to apprise Czentovic how little a further pursuit of our dilettantish striving was
worthy of his expert interest. With the same matter-of-
course gesture with which one of us disposes of a poor de-
tective story that has been proffered in a bookstore—
without even thumbing its pages—he turned away from
our table and left the room. "Weighed in the balance and
found wanting," I thought and, slightly stung by the cool,
contemptuous look and to give vent to my ill humour in
some fashion, I said to MacIver, "Your move didn't seem
to impress the master."

"Which master?"

I told him that the man who had just walked by after
glancing disapprovingly at our game was Czentovic, international chess champion. And I added that we would
be able to survive it without taking his contempt too
greatly to heart; the poor have to cook with water. But to
my astonishment these idle words of mine produced quite
an unexpected result. Immediately he became excited,
forgot our game, and his ambition took to an almost
audible throbbing. He had no notion that Czentovic was
on board: Czentovic simply had to give him a game; the
only time he had ever played with a champion was in a
multiple game when he was one of forty; even that was
fearfully exciting, and he had come quite near winning. Did I know the champion personally?—I didn't.—
Would I not invite him to join us?—I declined on the
ground that I was aware of Czentovic's reluctance to
make new acquaintances. Besides, what charm would
intercourse with third-rate players hold for a champion?

It would have been just as well not to say that about third-rate players to a man of MacIver's brand of conceit. Annoyed, he leaned back and declared gruffly that, as for himself, he couldn't believe that Czentovic would decline a gentleman's courteous challenge; he'd see to that. Upon getting a brief description of the master's person he stormed out, indifferent to our unfinished game, uncontrollably impatient to intercept Czentovic on the deck. Again I sensed that there was no holding the possessor of such broad shoulders once his will was involved in an undertaking.

I waited, somewhat tensed. Some ten minutes elapsed and MacIver returned, not in too good humour, it seemed to me.

"Well?" I asked.

"You were right," he answered, a bit annoyed. "Not a very pleasant gentleman. I introduced myself and told him who I am. He didn't even put out his hand. I tried to make him understand that all of us on board would be proud and honoured if he'd play the lot of us. But he was cursed stiff-necked about it; said he was sorry but his contractual obligations to his agent definitely precluded any game during his entire tour except for a fee. And his minimum is $250 per game."

I had to laugh. The thought would never have come to me that one could make so much money by pushing figures from black squares to white ones. "Well, I hope that you took leave of him with courtesy equal to his."

MacIver, however, remained perfectly serious. "The match is to come off at three tomorrow afternoon. Here in the smoking-room. I hope he won't make mincemeat of us easily."

"What! You promised him the $250?" I cried, quite taken aback.

"Why not? It's his business. If I had a toothache and there happened to be a dentist aboard, I wouldn't expect him to extract my tooth for nothing. The man's right to ask a fat price; in every line the big shots are the best traders. As far as I'm concerned, the less complicated the business, the better. I'd rather pay in cash than have your Mr. Czentovic do me a favour and in the end have to say 'thank you.' Anyway, many an evening at the club has cost me more than $250 without giving me a chance to play a world champion. It's no disgrace for a third-rate player to be beaten by a Czentovic."

It amused me to note how deeply I had injured Mac-Iver's self-love with that "third-rate." But as he was disposed to foot the bill for this expensive flyer, it was not for me to remark on his wounded ambition which promised at last to afford me an acquaintance with my odd fish. Promptly we notified the four or five others who had revealed themselves as chess players of the approaching event and reserved not only our own table but the adjacent ones so that we might suffer the least possible disturbance from passengers strolling by.

Next day all of our group was assembled at the appointed hour. The centre seat opposite that of the master was allotted to MacIver as a matter of course; his nervousness found outlet in the smoking of strong cigars which followed one after another and in restlessly glancing ever and again at the clock. The champion let us wait a good ten minutes—my friend's tale prompted the surmise that something like this would happen—thus heightening the impressiveness of his entry. He approached the table calmly and imperturbably. He offered no greeting— "You know who I am and I'm not interested in who you are" was what his discourtesy seemed to imply—but began in a dry, business-like way to lay down the conditions. Since there were not enough boards on the ship for separate games he proposed that we play against him collectively. After each of his moves he would retire to the end of the room so that his presence might not affect our consultations. As soon as our countermove had been made we were to strike a glass with a spoon, no table-bell being available. He proposed, if it pleased us, ten minutes as the maximum time for each move. Like timid pupils we accepted every suggestion unquestioningly. Czentovic drew black at the choice of colours; while still standing he made the first countermove, then turned at once to go to the designated waiting-place where he reclined lazily while carelessly examining an illustrated magazine.

There is little point in reporting the game. It ended, as it could not but end, in our complete defeat, and by the twenty-fourth move at that. There was nothing particularly astonishing about an international champion wiping off half a dozen mediocre or sub-mediocre players with his left hand; what served to disgust us, though, was the lordly manner with which Czentovic caused us to feel, all too plainly, that it was with his left hand that we had been disposed of. Each time he would give a quick, seemingly careless look at the board, and would look indolently past us as if we ourselves were dead wooden figures; and this impertinent proceeding reminded one irresistibly of the way one throws a mangy dog a morsel without taking the trouble to look at him. According to my way of thinking, if he had any sensitivity he might have shown us our mistakes or cheered us up with a friendly word. Even at the conclusion this sub-human chess automaton uttered no syllable, but, after saying "mate," stood motionless at the table waiting to ascertain whether another game was desired. I had already risen with the thought of indicating by a gesture—helpless as one always remains in the face of thick-skinned rudeness—that as far as I was concerned the pleasure of our acquaintance was ended now that the dollars-and-cents part of it was over, when, to my anger, MacIver, next to me, spoke up hoarsely: "Revanche!"

The note of challenge startled me; MacIver at this moment seemed much more like a pugilist about to put up his fists than a polite gentleman. Whether it was Czentovic's disagreeable treatment of us that affected him or merely MacIver's own pathological irritable ambition, suffice it that the latter's being had undergone a complete change. Red in the face up to his hair, his nostrils taut from inner pressure, he breathed hard and a sharp fold separated the bitten lips from his belligerently projected jaw. I recognized, disquieted, that flicker of the eyes that connotes uncontrollable passion, such as seizes only players at roulette when the right colour fails to come after the sixth or seventh successively doubled stake. Instantly I knew that this fanatical climber would, even at the cost of his entire fortune, play against Czentovic and play and play and play, for simple or doubled stakes, until he won at least a single game. If Czentovic stuck to it, MacIver would prove a gold-mine which would yield him a nice few thousands by the time Buenos Aires came in sight.

Czentovic remained unmoved. "If you please," he responded politely, "you gentlemen will take black this time."

There was nothing different about the second game except that our group became larger because of a few added onlookers, and livelier, too. MacIver stared fixedly at the board as if he willed to magnetize the chess-men to victory; I sensed that he would have paid a thousand dollars with delight if he could but shout "Mate" at our cold-snouted adversary. Oddly enough, something of his sullen excitement entered unconsciously into all of us. Every single move was discussed with greater emotion than before; always we would wrangle up to the last moment before agreeing to signal Czentovic to return to the table. We had come to the seventeenth move and, to our own surprise, entered on a combination which seemed staggeringly advantageous because we had been enabled to advance a pawn to the last square but one; we needed but to move it forward to c_1 to win a second queen. Not that we felt too comfortable about so obvious an opportunity; we were united in suspecting that the advantage which we seemed to have wrested could be no more than bait dangled by Czentovic whose vision enabled him to view the situation from a distance of several moves. Yet in spite of common examination and discussion, we were unable to explain it as a feint. At last, at the limit of our ten minutes, we decided to risk the move. MacIver's fingers were on the pawn to move it to the last square when he felt his arm gripped and heard a voice, low and impetuous, whisper, "For God's sake! Don't!"

Involuntarily we all turned about. I recognized in the man of some forty-five years, who must have joined the group during the last few minutes in which we were

absorbed in the problem before us, one whose narrow
sharp face had already arrested my attention on deck
strolls because of its extraordinary, almost chalky pal-
lor. Conscious of our gaze he continued rapidly:

"If you make a queen he will immediately attack with
the bishop, then you'll take it with your knight. Meantime, however, he moves his pawn to d7, threatens your
rook, and even if you check with the knight you're lost
and will be wiped out in nine or ten moves. It's prac-
tically the constellation that Alekhin introduced when
he played Boguljobov in 1922 at the championship tournament at Pistany."

Astonished, MacIver released the pawn and, like the
rest of us, stared amazedly at the man who had descended
in our midst like a rescuing angel. Any one who can
reckon a mate nine moves ahead must necessarily be a
first-class expert, perhaps even a contestant now on his
way to the tournament to seize the championship, so
that his sudden presence, his thrust into the game at precisely the critical moment, partook almost of the super-
natural.

MacIver was the first to collect himself. "What do you
advise?" he asked suppressedly.

"Don't advance yet; rather a policy of evasion. First of
all, get the king out of the danger line from g8 to h7.
Then he'll probably transfer his attack to the other flank.
Then you parry that with the rook, c8 to c4; two moves
and he will have lost not only a pawn but his superiority,
and if you maintain your defensive properly you may be
able to make it a draw. That's the best you can get out
of it."

We gasped amazed. The precision no less than the
rapidity of his calculations dizzied us; it was as if he had

been reading the moves from a printed page. For all that, this unsuspected turn by which, thanks to his cutting in, the contest with a world champion promised a draw, worked wonders. Animated by a single thought, we moved aside so as not to obstruct his observation of the board.

Again MacIver inquired: "The king, then; to h7?"

"Surely. The main thing is to duck."

MacIver obeyed and we rapped on the glass. Czentovic came forward at his habitual even pace, his eyes swept the board and took in the countermove. Then he moved the pawn h2 to h4 on the king's flank exactly as our unknown aid had predicted. Already the latter was whispering excitedly:

"The rook forward, the rook, to c4; then he'll first have to cover the pawn. That won't help him, though. Don't bother about his pawns but attack with the knight c3 to d5, and the balance is again restored. Press the offensive instead of defending."

We had no idea of what he meant. He might have been talking Chinese. But once under his spell MacIver did as he had been bidden. Again we struck the glass to recall Czentovic. This was the first time that he made no quick decision; instead he looked fixedly at the board. His eyebrows contracted involuntarily. Then he made his move, the one which our stranger had said he would, and turned to go. Yet before he started off something novel and unexpected happened. Czentovic raised his eyes and surveyed our ranks; plainly he wanted to ascertain who it was that offered such unaccustomed energetic resistance.

Beginning with this moment our excitement grew immeasurably. Thus far we had played without genuine hope, but now every pulse beat hotly at the thought of breaking Czentovic's cold disdain. Without loss of time our new friend had directed the next move and we were ready to call Czentovic back. My fingers trembled as I hit the spoon against the glass. And now we registered our first triumph. Czentovic, who hitherto had executed his purpose standing, hesitated, hesitated and finally sat down. He did this slowly and heavily, but that was enough to cancel—in a physical sense if in no other—the difference in levels that had previously obtained. We had necessitated his acknowledgment of equality, spatially at least. He cogitated long, his eyes resting immovably on the board so that one could scarcely discern the pupils under the heavy lids, and under the strained application his mouth opened gradually, which gave him a rather foolish look. Czentovic reflected for some minutes, then made a move and rose. At once our friend said half audibly:

"A stall! Well thought out! But don't yield to it! Force an exchange, he's got to exchange, then we'll get a draw and not even the gods can help him."

MacIver did as he was told. The succeeding manœuvres between the two men—we others had long since become mere supernumeraries—consisted of a back-and-forth that we were unable to comprehend. After some seven moves Czentovic looked up after a period of silence and said, "Draw."

For a moment a total stillness reigned. Suddenly one heard the rushing of the waves and the jazzing radio in the adjacent drawing-room; one picked out every step on the promenade outside and the faint thin susurration of the wind that carried through the window-frames. None of us breathed; it had come upon us too abruptly and we were nothing less than frightened in the face of the impossible: that this stranger should have been able to force his will on the world champion in a contest already half lost. MacIver shoved himself back and relaxed, and his suppressed breathing became audible in the joyous "Ah" that passed his lips. I took another look at Czentovic. It had already seemed to me during the later moves that he grew paler. But he understood how to maintain his poise. He persisted in his apparent imperturbability and asked, in a negligent tone, the while he pushed the figures off the board with a steady hand:

"Would you like to have a third game, gentlemen?"

The question was matter-of-fact, just business. What was note-worthy was that he ignored MacIver and looked straight and intently into the eyes of our rescuer. Just as a horse takes a new rider's measure by the firmness of his seat, he must have become cognizant of who was his real, in fact his only, opponent. We could not help but follow his gaze and look eagerly at the unknown. However, before he could collect himself and formulate an answer, MacIver, in his eager excitement, had already cried to him in triumph:

"Certainly, no doubt about it! But this time you've got to play him alone! You against Czentovic!"

What followed was quite extraordinary. The stranger, who curiously enough was still staring with a strained expression at the bare board, became affrighted upon hearing the lusty call and perceiving that he was the centre of observation. He looked confused.

"By no means, gentlemen," he said haltingly, plainly perplexed. "Quite out of the question. You'll have to leave me out. It's twenty, no, twenty-five years since I sat at a chess-board and . . . and I'm only now conscious of my bad manners in crashing your game without so much as a by your leave. . . . Please excuse my presumption. I don't want to interfere further." And before we could recover from our astonishment he had left us and gone out.

"But that's just impossible!" boomed the irascible Mac-Iver, pounding with his fist. "Out of the question that this fellow hasn't played chess for twenty-five years. Why, he calculated every move, every countermove, five or six in advance. You can't shake that out of your sleeve. Just out of the question—isn't it?"

Involuntarily, MacIver turned to Czentovic with the last question. But the champion preserved his unalterable frigidity.

"It's not for me to express an opinion. In any case there was something queer and interesting about the man's game; that's why I purposely left him a chance."

With that he rose lazily and added, in his objective manner: "If he or you gentlemen should want another game tomorrow, I'm at your disposal from three o'clock on."

We were unable to suppress our chuckles. Every one of us knew that the chance which Czentovic had allowed his nameless antagonist had not been prompted by generosity and that the remark was no more than a childish ruse to cover his frustration. It served to stimulate the more actively our desire to witness the utter humbling of so unshakable an arrogance. All at once we peaceable, indolent seagoers were seized by a mad, ambitious will to battle, for the thought that just on our ship, in mid ocean, the palm might be wrested from the champion—a record that would be flashed to every news bureau in the world—fascinated us challengingly. Added to that was the lure of the mysterious which emanated from the unexpected entry of our saviour at the crucial instant, and the contrast between his almost painful modesty and the rigid self-consciousness of the professional. Who was this unknown? Had destiny utilized this opportunity to command the revelation of a yet undiscovered chess phenomenon? Or was it that we were dealing with an expert who, for some undisclosed reason, craved anonymity? We discussed these various possibilities excitedly; the most extreme hypotheses were not sufficiently extreme to reconcile the stranger's puzzling shyness with his surprising declaration in the face of his demonstrated mastery. On one point, however, we were of one mind: to forgo no chance of a renewal of the contest. We resolved to exert ourselves to the limit to induce our godsend to play Czentovic the next day, MacIver pledging himself to foot the bill. Having in the meantime learned from the steward that the unknown was an Austrian, I, as his compatriot, was delegated to present our request.

Soon I found our man reclining in his deck-chair, reading. In the moment of approach I used the opportunity to observe him. The sharply chiselled head rested on the cushion in a posture of slight exhaustion; again I was struck by the extraordinary colourlessness of the comparatively youthful face framed at the temples by glistening white hair, and I got the impression, I cannot say why, that this person must have aged suddenly. No sooner did I stand before him than he rose courteously and introduced himself by a name that was familiar to me as belonging to a highly respected family of old Austria. I remembered that a bearer of that name had been an intimate friend of Schubert, and that one of the old

Emperor's physicians-in-ordinary had belonged to the same family. Dr. B. was visibly dumbfounded when I stated our wish that he take Czentovic on. It proved that he had no idea that he had stood his ground against a champion, let alone the most famous one in the world at the moment. For some reason this news seemed to make a special impression on him, for he inquired once and again whether I was sure that his opponent was truly a recognized holder of international honours. I soon perceived that this circumstance made my mission easier, but sensing his refined feelings, I considered it discreet to withhold the fact that MacIver would be a pecuniary loser in case of an eventual defeat. After considerable hesitation Dr. B. at last consented to a match but with the proviso that my fellow-players be warned against putting extravagant hope in his expertness.

"Because," he added with a clouded smile, "I really don't know whether I have the ability to play the game according to all the rules. I assure you that it was not by any means false modesty that made me say that I hadn't touched a chess-man since my college days, say more than twenty years. And even then I had no particular gifts as a player."

This was said so simply that I had not the slightest doubt of its truth. And yet I could not but express wonderment at his accurate memory of the details of positions in games by many different masters; he must, at least, have been greatly occupied with chess theory. Dr. B. smiled once more in that dreamy way of his.

"Greatly occupied! Heaven knows, it's true enough that I have occupied myself with chess greatly. But that happened under quite special, I might say unique, circumstances. The story of it is rather complicated and it might go as a little chapter in the story of our agreeable epoch. Do you think you would have patience for half an hour . . . ?"

He waved towards the deck-chair next to his. I accepted the invitation gladly. There were no near neighbours. Dr. B. removed his reading spectacles, laid them to one side, and began.

"You were kind enough to say that, as a Viennese, you remembered the name of my family. I am pretty sure, however, that you could hardly have heard of the law office which my father and I conducted—and later I alone—for we had no cases that got into the papers and we avoided new clients on principle. In truth, we no longer had a regular law practice but confined ourselves exclusively to advising, and mainly to administering the fortunes of the great monasteries with which my father, once a Deputy of the Clerical Party, was closely connected. Besides—in this day and generation I am no longer obliged to keep silence about the Monarchy—we had been entrusted with the investment of the funds of certain members of the Imperial family. These connexions with the Court and the Church—my uncle had been the Emperor's household physician, another was an abbot in Seitenstetten—dated back two generations; all that we had to do was to maintain them, and the task allotted to us through this inherited confidence—a quiet, I might almost say a soundless, task—really called for little more than strict discretion and dependability, two qualities which my late father possessed in full measure; he succeeded, in fact, through his prudence in preserving considerable values for his clients through the years of inflation as well as the period of collapse. Then when

Hitler seized the helm in Germany and began to raid the properties of churches and cloisters, certain negotiations and transactions, initiated from the other side of the frontier with a view to saving at least the movable valuables from confiscation, went through our hands and we two knew more about sundry secret transactions between the Curia and the Imperial house than the public will ever learn of. But the very inconspicuousness of our office —we hadn't even a sign on the door—as well as the care with which both of us almost ostentatiously kept out of Monarchist circles, offered the safest protection from officious investigations. In fact, no Austrian official had ever suspected that during all those years the secret couriers of the Imperial family delivered and fetched their most important mail in our unpretentious fourth floor office.

"It happens that the National Socialists began, long before they armed their forces against the world, to organize a different but equally schooled and dangerous army in all contiguous countries—the legion of the unprivileged, the despised, the injured. Their so-called 'cells' nested themselves in every office, in every business; they had listening-posts and spies in every spot, right up to the private chambers of Dollfuss and Schuschnigg. They had their man, as alas! I learned only too late, even in our insignificant office. True, he was nothing but a wretched, ungifted clerk whom I had engaged on the recommendation of a priest for no other purpose than to give the office the appearance of a going concern; all that we really used him for was innocent errands, answering the telephone, and filing papers, that is to say papers of no real importance. He was not allowed to open the mail. I typed important letters myself and kept no copies. I took all essential documents to my home and I held private interviews nowhere but in the priory of the cloister or in my uncle's consultation room. These measures of caution prevented the listening-post from seeing anything that went on, but some unlucky happening must have made the vain and ambitious fellow aware that he was mistrusted and that interesting things were going on behind his back. It may have been that in my absence one of the couriers made a careless reference to 'His Majesty' instead of the stipulated 'Baron Fern,' or that the rascal opened letters surreptitiously; anyhow, before I had ground for suspicion, he managed to get a mandate from Berlin or Munich to watch us. It was only much later, long after my imprisonment began, that I remembered how his early laziness at work had changed in the last few months to a sudden eagerness when he frequently offered, almost intrusively, to post my letters. I cannot acquit myself of a certain amount of imprudence, but after all, haven't the greatest diplomats and generals of the world, too, been out-manœuvred by Hitler's cunning? Just how precisely and lovingly the Gestapo had long been directing its attention to me was manifested tangibly by the fact that the SS people arrested me on the evening of the very day of Schuschnigg's abdication and a day before Hitler entered Vienna. Luckily I had been able to burn the most important documents upon hearing Schuschnigg's farewell address over the radio, and the other papers, along with the indispensable vouchers for the securities held abroad for the cloisters and two archdukes, I concealed in a basket of laundry which my faithful housekeeper took to my uncle. All of this almost literally in the last minute before the fellows stove my door in."

Dr. B. interrupted himself long enough to light a cigar. I noticed by the light of the match a nervous twitch at the right corner of his mouth that had struck me before and which, as far as I could observe, recurred every few minutes. It was merely a fleeting vibration, hardly stronger than a breath, but it imparted to the whole face a singular restlessness.

"I suppose you expect that I'm going to tell you about the concentration camp to which all who held faith with our old Austria were removed, about the degradations, martyrings and tortures that I suffered there. Nothing of the kind happened. I was in a different category. I was not put with those luckless ones on whom they released their accumulated resentment by corporal and spiritual degradation, but rather was assigned to that small group out of which the National Socialists hoped to squeeze money or important information. My obscure person in itself meant nothing to the Gestapo, of course. They must have guessed, though, that we were the dummies, the administrators and confidants, of their most embittered adversaries, and what they expected to compel from me was incriminating evidence, evidence against the monasteries to support charges of violation by those who had selflessly taken up the cudgels for the Monarchy. They suspected, and not without good reason, that a substantial portion of the funds that we handled was still secreted and inaccessible to their lust for loot—hence their choice of me on the very first day in order to force the desired information by their trusted methods. That is why persons of my sort, to whom they looked for money or significant evidence, were not dumped into a concentration camp but were sorted out for special handling. You will recall that our Chancellor, and also Baron

Rothschild from whose family they hoped to extort millions, were not planted behind barbed wire in a prison camp but, ostensibly privileged, were lodged in individual rooms in a hotel, the Metropole, which happened to be the Gestapo headquarters. The same distinction was bestowed on my insignificant self.

"A room to oneself in a hotel—sounds pretty decent, doesn't it? But you may believe me that they had not in mind decenter but a more crafty technique when, instead of stuffing us 'prominent' ones in blocks of twenty into icy barracks, they housed us in tolerably heated hotel rooms, each by himself. For the pressure by which they planned to compel the needed testimony was to be exerted more subtly than through common beating or physical torture: by the most conceivably complete isolation. They did nothing to us; they merely deposited us in the midst of nothing, knowing well that of all things the most potent pressure on the soul of man is nothingness. By placing us singly, each in an utter vacuum, in a chamber that was hermetically closed to the world without, it was calculated that the pressure created from inside, rather than cold and the scourge, would eventually cause our lips to spring apart.

The first sight of the room allotted to me was not at all repellent. There was a door, a table, a bed, a chair, a wash-basin, a barred window. The door, however, remained closed night and day; the table remained bare of book, newspaper, pencil, paper; the window gave on a brick wall; my ego and my physical self were contained in a structure of nothingness. They had taken every object from me: the watch that I might not know the hour, the pencil that I might not make a note, the pocket-knife that I might not sever a vein; even the slight narcotic of a cigarette was forbidden me. Except for the warder, who was not permitted to address me or to answer a question, I saw no human face, I heard no human voice; from dawn to night there was no sustenance for eye or ear or any sense; one was alone with oneself, with one's body and four or five inanimate things, rescuelessly alone with table, bed, window, and basin; one lived like a diver in his bell in the black ocean of this silence—like a diver, too, who is dimly aware that the cable to safety has already snapped and that he never will be raised from the soundless depths. There was nothing to do, nothing to hear, nothing to see; about one, everywhere and without interruption, there was nothingness, emptiness without space or time. One walked to and fro, and with one went one's thoughts, to and fro, to and fro, ever again. But even thoughts, insubstantial as they seem, require an anchorage if they are not to revolve and circle around themselves; they too weigh down under nothingness. One waited for something from morn to eve and nothing happened. Nothing happened. One waited, waited, waited; one thought, one thought, one thought until one's temples smarted. Nothing happened. One remained alone. Alone. Alone.

"That lasted for a fortnight during which I lived outside of time, outside the world. If war had broken out then I would never have discovered it, for my world comprised only table, door, bed, basin, chair, window and wall, every line of whose scallopped pattern imbedded itself as with a steel graver in the innermost folds of my brain every time it met my eye. Then, at last, the hearings began. Suddenly one received a summons; one hardly knew whether it was day or night. One was called and led through a few corridors, one knew not whither;

then one waited and knew not where it was, and found oneself standing at a table behind which some uniformed men were seated. Piles of papers on the table, documents of whose contents one was in ignorance; and then came the questions, the real ones and the false, the simple and the cunning, the catch questions and the dummy questions, and whilst one answered strange and evil fingers toyed with papers whose contents one could not surmise, and strange evil fingers wrote a record and one could not know what they wrote. But the most fearsome thing for me at those hearings was that I never could guess or figure out what the Gestapo actually knew about the goings on in my office and what they sought to worm out of me. I have already told you that at the last minute I gave my housekeeper the really incriminating documents to take to my uncle. Had he received them? Had he not received them? How far had I been betrayed by that clerk? Which letters had they intercepted and what might they not already have screwed out of some clumsy priest at one of the cloisters which we represented?

"And they heaped question on question. What securities had I bought for this cloister, with which banks had I corresponded, do I know Mr. So-and-so or do I not, had I corresponded with Switzerland and with God-knows where? And not being able to divine what they had already dug up, every answer was fraught with danger. Were I to admit something that they didn't know I might be unnecessarily exposing somebody to the axe. If I denied too much I harmed myself.

"The worst was not the examination. The worst was the return from the examination to my void, to the same room with the same table, the same bed, the same basin, the same wall-paper. No sooner was I by myself than I

tried to recapitulate, to think of what I should have said
and what I should say next time so as to divert the suspicion that a careless remark of mine might have
aroused. I pondered, I combed through, I probed, I ap-
praised every single word of testimony before the examining office. I restated their every question and every
answer that I made. I sought to sift out the part that went
into the protocol, knowing well that it was all incalcula-
ble and unascertainable. But these thoughts, once given
rein in empty space, rotated in my head unceasingly, always starting afresh in ever-changing combinations and
insinuating themselves into my sleep.

"After every hearing by the Gestapo my own thoughts
took over no less inexorably the martyrizing questions,
searchings and torments, and perhaps even more horri-
bly, for the hearings at least ended after an hour, but this
repetition, thanks to the spiteful torture of solitude,
never. And always the table, chest, bed, wall-paper, window; no diversion, not a book or magazine, not a new
face, no pencil with which to jot down an item, not a
match to toy with—nothing, nothing, nothing. It was
only at this point that I apprehended how devilishly in-
telligently, with what murderous psychology, this hotel-
room system was conceived. In a concentration camp one
would, perhaps, have had to wheel rocks until one's
hands bled and one's feet froze in one's boots; one would
have been packed in stench and cold with a couple of
dozen others. But one would have seen faces, would have
had space, a tree, a star, something, anything, to stare at,
while here everything stood before one unchangeably the
same, always the same, maddeningly the same. There was
nothing here to switch me off from my thoughts, from my
delusive notions, from my diseased recapitulating. That

was just what they purposed: they wanted me to gag and gag on my thoughts until they choked me and I had no choice but to spit them out at last, to admit—admit everything that they were after, finally to yield up the evidence and the people.

"I gradually became aware of how my nerves were slacking under the grisly pressure of the void and, conscious of the danger, I tensed my nerves to the bursting point in an effort to find or create any sort of diversion. I tried to recite or reconstruct everything that I had ever memorized in order to occupy myself—the folk songs and nursery rhymes of childhood, the Homer of my high-school days, clauses from the Civil Code. Then I did problems in arithmetic, adding or dividing, but my memory was powerless without some integrating force. I was unable to concentrate on anything. One thought flickered and darted about: how much do they know? What is it that they don't know? What did I say yesterday —what ought I to say next time?

"This simply indescribable state lasted four months. Well, four months; easy to write, just about a dozen letters! Easy to say, too: four months, a couple of syllables. The lips can articulate the sound in a quarter of a second: four months. But nobody can describe or measure or demonstrate, not to another or to himself, how long a period endures in the spaceless and timeless, nor can one explain to another how it eats into and destroys one, this nothing and nothing and nothing that is all about, everlastingly this table and bed and basin and wall-paper, and always that silence, always the same warder who shoves the food in without looking at one, always those same thoughts that revolve around one in the nothing-ness, until one becomes insane.

"Small signs made me disturbedly conscious that my brain was not working right. Early in the game my mind had been quite clear at the examinations; I had testified quietly and deliberately; my twofold thinking—what should I say and what not?—had still functioned. Now I could no more than articulate haltingly the simplest sentences, for while I spoke my eyes were fixed in a hypnotic stare on the pen that sped recordingly across the paper as if I wished to race after my own words. I felt myself losing my grip, I felt that the moment was coming closer and closer when, to rescue myself, I would tell all I knew and perhaps more; when, to elude the strangling grip of that nothingness, I would betray twelve persons and their secrets without deriving any advantage myself but the respite of a single breath.

"One evening I really reached that limit: the warder had just served my meal at such a moment of desperation when I suddenly shrieked after him: 'Take me to the board! I'll tell everything! I want to confess! I'll tell them where the papers are and where the money is! I'll tell them everything! Everything!' Fortunately he was far enough away not to hear me. Or perhaps he didn't want to hear me.

"An event occurred in this extremest need, something unforeseeable, that offered rescue, rescue if only for a period. It was late in July, a dark, ominous, rainy day: I recall these details quite definitely because the rain was rattling against the windows of the corridor through which I was being led to the examination. I had to wait in the ante-room of the hearing chamber. Always one had to wait before the session; the business of letting one wait was a trick of the game. They would first rip one's nerves by the call, the abrupt summons from the cell in the mid-

dle of the night, and then, by the time one was keyed to
the ordeal with will and reason tensed to resistance, they
caused one to wait, meaningless meaningful waiting, an
hour, two hours, three hours before the trial, to weary
the body and humble the spirit. And they caused me to
wait particularly long on this Thursday, the 27th of July;
twice the hour struck while I attended, standing, in the
ante-room; there is a special reason, too, for my remem-
bering the date so exactly.

"A calendar hung in this room—it goes without saying
that they never permitted me to sit down; my legs bored
into my body for two hours—and I find it impossible to
convey to you how my hunger for something printed,
something written, made me stare at these figures, these
few words, '27 July,' against the wall; I wolfed them into
my brain. Then I waited some more and waited and
looked to see when the door would open at last, meanwhile reflecting on what my inquisitors might ask me
this time, knowing well that they would ask me something quite different from that for which I was schooling
myself. Yet in the face of all that, the torment of the waiting and standing was nevertheless a blessing, a delight,
because this room was, after all, a different one than my
own, somewhat larger and with two windows instead of
one, and without the bed and without the basin and
without that crack in the window-sill that I had regarded
a million times. The door was painted differently, a different chair stood against the wall, and to the left stood
a filing cabinet with documents as well as a clothes-stand
on which three or four wet military coats hung—my torturers' coats. So that I had something new, something
different to look at, at last something different for my
starved eyes, and they clawed greedily at every detail.

"I took in every fold of those garments; I observed, for example, a drop suspended from one of the wet collars and, ludicrous as it may sound to you, I waited in an inane excitement to see whether the drop would eventually detach itself and roll down or whether it would resist gravity and stay put; truly, this drop held me breathless for minutes, as if my life had been at stake. It rolled down after all, and then I counted the buttons on the coats again, eight on one, eight on another, ten on the third, and again I compared the insignia; all of these absurd and unimportant trifles toyed with, teased, and pinched my hungry eyes with an avidity which I forgo trying to describe. And suddenly I saw something that paralysed my gaze. I had discovered a slight bulge in the side-pocket of one of the coats. I moved closer to it and thought that I recognized, by the rectangular shape of the protrusion, what this swollen pocket harboured: a book! My knees trembled: a *book!*

"I hadn't had a book in my hand for four months, so that the mere idea of a book in which words appear in orderly arrangement, of sentences, pages, leaves, a book in which one could follow and stow in one's brain new, unknown, diverting thoughts, was at once intoxicating and stupefying. Hypnotized, my eyes rested on the little swelling which the book inside the pocket formed; they glowered at the spot as if to burn a hole in the coat. The moment came when I could no longer control my greed; involuntarily I edged nearer. The mere thought that my hands might at least feel the book through the cloth made the nerves of my fingers tingle to the nails. Almost without knowing what I did I found myself getting closer to it.

"Happily the warder ignored my surely singular behaviour; indeed, it may have seemed to him quite natural that a man wanted to lean against a wall after standing erect for two hours. And then I was quite close to the coat, my hands purposely clasped behind me so as to be able to touch the coat unnoticed. I felt the stuff and the contact confirmed that here was something square, something flexible, and that it crackled softly—a book, a book! And then a thought went through me like a shot: steal the book! If you can turn the trick, you can hide the book in your cell and read, read, read—read again at last. The thought, hardly lodged in me, operated like a strong poison; at once there was a singing in my ears, my heart hammered, my hands froze and resisted my bidding. But after that first numbness I pressed myself softly and insinuatingly against the coat; I pressed—always fixing the warder with my eye—the book up out of the pocket, higher and higher, with my artfully concealed hands. Then: a tug, a gentle, careful pull, and in no time the little book, small in format, was in my hand. Not until now was I frightened at my deed. Retreat was no longer possible. What to do with it? I shoved the book under my trousers at the back just far enough for the belt to hold it, then gradually to the hip so that while walking I could keep it in place by holding my hands on the trouser-seams, military fashion. I had to try it out so I moved a step from the clothes-rack, two steps, three steps. It worked. It was possible to keep the book in place while walking if I but kept pressing firmly against my belt.

"Then came the hearing. It demanded greater attention than ever on my part, for while answering I concentrated my entire effort on securing the book inconspicuously rather than on my testimony. Luckily this session proved to be a short one and I got the book safely to my room, though it slipped into my trousers most danger-ously while in the corridor on my way back and I had to simulate a violent fit of coughing as an excuse for bend-ing over to get it under my belt again. But what a mo-ment, that, as I bore it back into my inferno, alone at last yet no longer alone!

"You will suppose, of course, that my first act was to seize the book, examine it and read it. Not at all! I wanted, first of all, to savour the joy of possessing a book; the artificially prolonged and nerve-inflaming desire to day-dream about the kind of book I would wish this stolen one to be: above all, very small type, narrowly spaced, with many, many letters, many, many thin leaves so that it might take long to read. And then I wished to myself that it might be one that would demand mental exertion, nothing smooth or light; rather something from which I could learn and memorize, preferably—oh, what an audacious dream!—Goethe or Homer. At last I could no longer check my greed and my curiosity. Stretched on the bed so as to arouse no suspicion in case the warder might open the door without warning, trem-blingly I drew the volume from under my belt.

"The first glance produced not merely disappointment but a sort of bitter vexation, for this booty, whose ac-quirement was surrounded with such monstrous danger and such glowing hope, proved to be nothing more than a chess anthology, a collection of one hundred and fifty championship games. Had I not been barred, locked in, I would, in my first rage, have thrown the thing through an open window; for what was to be done—what could be done—with nonsense of the kind? Like most of the other boys at school I had now and then tried my hand at chess to kill time. But of what use was this theoretical stuff to me? You can't play chess alone, and certainly not without chess-men and a board. Annoyed, I thumbed the pages thinking to discover reading matter of some sort, an introduction, a manual; but, besides the bare rectangular reproductions of the various master games with their symbols—*a1-a2, Kt.-f1-Kt.-g3*, etc.—to me then unintelligible, I found nothing. All of it appeared to me as a kind of algebra the key to which was hidden. Only gradually I puzzled out that the letters a, b, c stood for the vertical rows, the figures 1 to 8 for the rows across, and indicated the current position of each figure; thus these purely graphic expressions did, nevertheless, attain to speech.

"Who knows, I thought, if I were able to devise a chess-board in my cell I could follow these games through; and it seemed like a sign from heaven that the weave of my bed-sheet disclosed a coarse checkering. With proper manipulation it yielded a field of sixty-four squares. I tore out the first leaf and concealed the book under my mattress. Then, from bits of bread that I sacrificed, I began to mould king, queen, and the other figures (with ludicrous results, of course), and after no end of effort I was finally able to undertake on the bed-sheet the reproduction of the positions pictured in the chess book. But my absurd bread-crumb figures, half of which I had covered with dust to differentiate them from 'white' ones, proved utterly inadequate when I tried to pursue the printed game. I was all confusion in those first days; I would have to start a game afresh five times, ten times, twenty times. But who on earth had so much unused and useless time as I, slave of emptiness, and who commanded so much immeasurable greed and patience!

"It took me six days to play the game to the end without an error, and in a week after that I no longer required the chess-men to comprehend the relative positions, and in just one more week I was able to dispense with the bed-sheet; the printed symbols, a1, a2, c7, c8, at first abstractions to me, automatically transformed themselves into visual plastic positions. The transposition had been accomplished perfectly. I had projected the chess-board and its figures within myself and, thanks to the bare rules, observed the immediate set-up just as a practised musician hears all instruments singly and in combination upon merely glancing at a printed score.

"It cost me no effort, after another fortnight, to play every game in the book from memory or, in chess language, blind; and only then did I begin to understand the limitless benefaction which my impertinent theft constituted. For I had acquired an occupation—a senseless, a purposeless one if you wish—yet one that negated the nothingness that enveloped me; the one hundred and fifty championship games equipped me with a weapon against the strangling monotony of space and time.

"From then on, to conserve the charm of this new interest without interruption, I divided my day precisely: two games in the morning, two in the afternoon, a quick recapitulation in the evening. That served to fill my day which previously had been as shapeless as jelly; I had something to do that did not tire me, for a wonderful feature of chess is that through confining mental energy to a strictly bounded field the brain does not flag even under the most strained concentration; rather it makes more acute its agility and energy. In the course of time the repetition of the master games, which had at first been mechanical, awaked an artistic, a pleasurable com-

prehension in me. I learned to understand the refine-
ments, the tricks and feints in attack and defence; I
grasped the technique of thinking ahead, planning combinations and riposting, and soon recognized the per-
sonal note of each champion in his individual method
as infallibly as one spots a particular poet on hearing only
a few lines. That which began as a mere time-killing occupation became a joy, and the personalities of such
great chess strategists as Alekhin, Lasker, Boguljobov
and Tartakover entered into my solitude as beloved comrades.

"My silent cell was constantly and variously peopled,
and the very regularity of my exercises restored my already impaired intellectual capacity; my brain seemed
refreshed and, because of constant disciplined thinking,
even keenly whetted. My ability to think more clearly
and concisely manifested itself, above all, at the hearings; unconsciously I had perfected myself at the chess-
board in defending myself against false threats and
masked dodges; from this time on I gave them no openings at the sessions and I even harboured the thought that
the Gestapo men began, after a while, to regard me with
a certain respect. Possibly they asked themselves, seeing
so many others collapse, from what secret sources I alone
found strength for such unshakable resistance.

"This period of happiness in which I played through
the one hundred and fifty games in that book systemati-
cally, day by day, continued for about two and one-half
to three months. Then I arrived unexpectedly at a dead
point. Suddenly I found myself once more facing nothingness. For by the time that I had played through each
one of these games innumerable times, the charm of nov-

elty and surprise was lost, the exciting and stimulating power was exhausted. What purpose did it serve to repeat again and again games whose every move I had long since memorized? No sooner did I make an opening move than the whole thing unravelled of itself; there was no surprise, no tension, no problem. At this point I would have needed another book with more games to keep me busy, to engage the mental effort that had become indispensable to divert me. This being totally impossible, my madness could take but one course: instead of the old games I had to devise new ones myself. I had to try to play the game with myself or, rather, against myself.

"I have no idea to what extent you have given thought to the intellectual status of this game of games. But one doesn't have to reflect deeply to see that if pure chance can determine a game of calculation, it is an absurdity in logic to play against oneself. The fundamental attraction of chess lies, after all, singly in that its strategy develops in different wise in two different brains, that in this mental battle Black, ignorant of White's immediate manœuvres, seeks constantly to guess and cross them while White, for his part, strives to penetrate Black's secret purposes and to outstrip and parry them. If one person tries to be both Black and White you have the preposterous situation that one and the same brain at once knows something and yet does not know it; that, functioning as White's partner, it can instantly obey a command to forget what, a moment earlier as Black's partner, it desired and plotted. Such cerebral duality really implies a complete cleavage of the conscious, a lighting up or dimming of the brain function at pleasure as with a switch; in short, to want to play against oneself at chess is about as paradoxical as to want to jump over one's own shadow.

"Well, briefly, in my desperation I tried this impossibility, this absurdity, for months. There was no choice but this nonsense if I was not to become quite insane or slowly to disintegrate mentally. The fearful state that I was in compelled me at least to attempt this split between Black ego and White ego so as not to be crushed by the horrible nothingness that bore in on me."

Dr. B. relaxed in his deck-chair and closed his eyes for a minute. It seemed as if he were exerting his will to suppress a disturbing recollection. Once again the left corner of his mouth twitched in that strange and evidently uncontrollable manner. Then he settled himself a little more erectly.

"Well, then, I hope I've made it all pretty intelligible up to this point. I'm sorry, but I doubt greatly that the rest of it can be pictured quite as clearly. This new occupation, you see, called for so unconditional a harnessing of the brain as to make any simultaneous self-control impossible. I have already intimated my opinion that a chess contest with oneself spells nonsense, but there is a minimal possibility for even such an absurdity if a real chess-board is present, because the board, being tangible, affords a sense of distance, a material extra-territoriality. Before a real chess-board with real chess-men you can stop to think things over, and you can place yourself physically first on this side of the table, then on the other, to fix in your eyes how the scene looks to Black and how it looks to White. Obliged as I was to conduct these contests against myself—or with myself, as you please—on an imaginary field, so I was obliged to keep fixedly in mind the current set-up on the sixty-four squares and, besides, not only the momentary status but to make advance calculations as to the possible further moves open to each player, which meant—I know how mad this must sound to you—imagining doubly, triply, no, imagining sextuply, duodecibly for each of my egos, always four or five moves in advance.

"Please don't think that I expect you to follow through the involutions of this madness. In these plays in the abstract space of fantasy I had to figure out the next four or five moves in my capacity of White, likewise as Black, thus considering every possible future combination with two brains, so to speak, White's brain and Black's brain. But even this auto-cleaving of personality was not the most dangerous aspect of my abstruse experiment; rather it was that with the need to play independently I lost my foothold and fell into a bottomless pit. The mere replaying of championship games, which I had been indulging in during the preceding weeks, had been, after all, no more than a feat of repetition, a straight recapitulation of given material and, as such, no greater strain than to memorize poetry or learn sections of the Civil Code by heart; it was a delimited, disciplined function and thus an excellent mental exercise. My two morning games, my two in the afternoon, represented a definite task that I was able to perform coolly; it was a substitute for normal occupation and, moreover, if I erred in the progress of a game or forgot the next move, I always had recourse to the book. It was only because the replaying of others' games left my self out of the picture that this activity served to soothe and heal my shattered nerves; it was all one to me whether Black or White was victor, for was it not Alekhin or Boguljobov who sought the palm, while my own person, my reason, my soul derived satisfaction as observer, as fancier of the niceties of those jousts as they worked out. From the moment at which I tried to play against myself I began, unconsciously, to challenge myself. Each of my egos, my Black ego and my White ego, had to contest against the other and became the centre, each on its own, of an ambition, an impatience to win, to conquer; after each move that I made as Ego Black, I was in a fever of curiosity as to what Ego White would do. Each of my egos felt triumphant when the other made a bad move and likewise suffered chagrin at similar clumsiness of its own.

"All that sounds senseless, and in fact such a self-produced schizophrenia, such a split consciousness with its fund of dangerous excitement would be unthinkable in a person under normal conditions. Don't forget, though, that I had been violently torn from all normality, innocently charged and behind bars, for months martyrized by the refined employment of solitude—a man seeking an object against which to discharge his long accumulated rage. And as I had nothing else than this insane match with myself, that rage, that lust for revenge, canalized itself fanatically into the game. Something in me wanted to justify itself, but there was only this other self with which I could wrestle; so while the game was on, an almost manic excitement waxed in me. In the beginning my deliberations were still quiet and composed; I would pause between one game and the next so as to recover from the effort; but little by little my frayed nerves forbade all respite. No sooner had Ego White made a move than Ego Black feverishly plunged a piece forward; scarcely had a game ended but I challenged myself to

another, for each time, of course, one of my chess-egos
was beaten by the other and demanded satisfaction.

"I shall never be able to tell, even approximately, how
many games I played against myself during those months
in my cell as a result of this crazy insatiability; a thousand
perhaps, perhaps more. It was an obsession against which
I could not arm myself; from dawn to night I thought of
nothing but knights and pawns, rooks and kings, and a
and b and c, and 'Mate!' and castle; my entire being and
every sense embraced the checkered board. The joy of
play became a lust for play; the lust for play became a
compulsion to play, a phrenetic rage, a mania which saturated not only my waking hours but eventually my sleep,
too. I could think only in terms of chess, only in chess
moves, chess problems; sometimes I would wake with a
damp brow and become aware that a game had unconsciously continued in my sleep, and if I dreamt of persons it was exclusively in the moves of the knight, the
rook, in the advance and retreat, of the knight's move.

"Even when I was brought before the hearing board
I was no longer able to keep my thoughts within the
bounds of my responsibilities; I'm inclined to think
that I must have expressed myself confusedly at the
last sessions for my judges would glance at one another
strangely. Actually I was merely waiting, while they
questioned and deliberated, in my cursed eagerness to
be led back to my cell so that I could resume my mad
round, to start a fresh game, and another and another.
Every interruption disturbed me; even the quarter hour
in which the warder cleaned up the room, the two minutes in which he served my meals, tortured my feverish impatience; sometimes the midday meal stood un-

touched on the tray at evening because the game made me forgetful of food. The only physical sensation that I experienced was a terrible thirst; the fever of this constant thinking and playing must already have manifested itself then; I emptied the bottle in two swallows and begged the warder for more, and nevertheless felt my tongue dry in my mouth in the next minute.

"Finally my excitement during the games rose—by that time I did nothing else from morning till night—to such a height that I was no longer able to sit still for a minute; uninterruptedly, while cogitating on a move, I would walk to and fro, quicker and quicker, to and fro, to and fro, and the nearer the approach to the decisive moment of the game the hotter my steps; the lust to win, to victory, to victory over myself increased to a sort of rage; I trembled with impatience, for the one chess-ego in me was always too slow for the other. One would whip the other forward and, absurd as this may seem to you, I would call angrily, 'Quicker, quicker!' or 'Go on, go on!' when the one self in me failed to riposte to the other's thrust quickly enough. It goes without saying that I am now fully aware that this state of mine was nothing less than a pathological form of overwrought mind for which I can find no other name than one not yet known to medical annals: chess poisoning.

"The time came when this monomania, this obsession, attacked my body as well as my brain. I lost weight, my sleep was restless and disturbed, upon waking I had to make great efforts to compel my leaden lids to open; sometimes I was so weak that when I grasped a glass I could scarcely raise it to my lips, my hands trembled so; but no sooner did the game begin than a mad power seized me: I rushed up and down, up and down with fists clenched, and I would sometimes hear my own voice as through a reddish fog, shouting hoarsely and angrily at myself, 'Check!' or 'Mate!'

"How this horrible, indescribable condition reached its crisis is something that I am unable to report. All that I know is that I woke one morning and the waking was different than usual. My body was no longer a burden, so to say; I rested softly and easily. A tight, agreeable fatigue, such as I had not known for months, lay on my eyelids; the feeling was so warm and benignant that I couldn't bring myself to open my eyes. For minutes I lay awake and continued to enjoy this heavy soddenness, this tepid reclining in agreeable stupefaction. All at once I seemed to hear voices behind me, living human voices, low whispering voices that spoke words; and you can't possibly imagine my delight, for months had elapsed, perhaps a year, since I had heard other words than the hard, sharp, evil ones from my judges. 'You're dreaming,' I said to myself. 'You're dreaming! Don't, under any circumstances, open your eyes. Let the dream last or you'll again see the cursed cell about you, the chair and washstand and the table and the wall-paper with the eternal pattern. You're dreaming—keep on dreaming!'

"But curiosity held the upper hand. Slowly and carefully I raised my lids. A miracle! It was a different room in which I found myself, a room wider and more ample than my hotel cell. An unbarred window admitted light freely and permitted a view of trees, green trees swaying in the wind, instead of my bald brick partition; the walls shone white and smooth, above me a high white ceiling; truly, I lay in a new and unaccustomed bed and—surely, it was no dream—human voices whispered behind me.

"In my surprise I must have made an abrupt, involun-

tary movement, for at once I heard an approaching step.
A woman came softly, a woman with a white head-dress,
a nurse, a Sister. A delighted shudder ran through me:
I had seen no woman for a year. I stared at the lovely apparition and it must have been a glance of wild ecstasy
for she admonished me, 'Quiet, don't move.' I hung only
on her voice, for was not this a person who talked! Was
there still somebody on earth who did not interrogate
me, torture me? And to top it all—ungraspable wonder!
—a soft, warm, almost tender woman's voice. I stared
hungrily at her mouth, for the year of inferno had made
it seem to me impossible that one person might speak
kindly to another. She smiled at me—yes, she smiled;
then there still were people who could smile benevo-
lently—put a warning finger to her lips, and went off
noiselessly. But I could not obey her order; I was not yet
sated with the miracle. I tried to wrench myself into a
sitting posture so as to follow with my eyes this wonder
of a human being who was kind. But when I reached out
to support my weight on the edge of the bed something
failed me. In place of my right hand, fingers, and wrist
I became aware of something foreign—a thick, large,
white cushion, obviously a comprehensive bandage. At
first I gaped uncomprehendingly at this bulky object,
then slowly I began to grasp where I was and to reflect
on what could have happened to me. They must have injured me, or I had done some damage to my hand myself.
The place was a hospital.

"The physician, an amiable elderly man, turned up at
noon. He knew who my family were and made so respectful an allusion to my uncle, the Imperial household doctor, as to create the impression that he was well disposed
to me. In the course of conversation he put all sorts of

questions to me, one of which, in particular, astonished me: Was I a mathematician or chemist? I answered in the negative.

" 'Strange,' he murmured. 'In your fever you cried out such unusual formulas, c_3, c_4. We could make nothing of it.'

"I asked him what had happened to me. He smiled oddly.

" 'Nothing too serious. An acute irritation of the nerves,' and added in a low voice, after looking carefully around him, 'and quite intelligible, of course. Let's see, it was March 13, wasn't it!'

"I nodded.

" 'No wonder, with that system,' he admitted. 'You're not the first. But don't worry.' The manner of his soothing speech and sympathetic smile convinced me that I was in a safe haven.

"A couple of days thereafter the doctor told me quite of his own accord what had taken place. The warder had heard shrieks from my cell and thought, at first, that I was disputing with somebody who had broken in. But no sooner had he shown himself at the door than I made for him, shouted wildly something that sounded like 'Aren't you ever going to move, you rascal, you coward?' grasped at his windpipe, and finally attacked him so ferociously that he had to call for help. Then when they were dragging me, in my mad rage, for medical examination, I had suddenly broken loose and thrust myself against the window in the corridor, thereby lacerating my hand—see this deep scar. I had been in a sort of brain fever during the first few days in the hospital, but now he found my perceptive faculties quite in order. 'To be sure,' said he under his voice, 'it's just as well that I don't report that higher up or they may still come and fetch you back there. Depend on me, I'll do my best.'

"Whatever it was that this benevolent doctor told my torturers about me is beyond my knowledge. In any case, he achieved what he sought to achieve: my release. It may be that he declared me irresponsible, or it may be that meanwhile my importance to the Gestapo had diminished, for Hitler had since occupied Bohemia, thus liquidating the case of Austria. I had merely to sign an undertaking to leave the country within a fortnight, and this period was so filled with the multitude of formalities that now surround a journey—military certificate, police, tax and health certificates, passport, visas—as to leave me no time to brood over the past. Apparently one's brain is controlled by secret, regulatory powers which automatically switch off whatever may annoy or endanger the mind, for every time I wanted to ponder on my imprisonment the light in my brain seemed to go off; only after many weeks, indeed only now, on this ship, did I pluck up enough courage to pass in review all that I lived through.

"After all this you will understand my unbecoming and perhaps strange conduct to your friends. It was only by chance that I was strolling through the smoking-room and saw them sitting at the chess-board; my feet seemed rooted where I stood from astonishment and fright. For I had totally forgotten that one can play chess with a real board and real figures, forgotten that two physically separate persons sit opposite each other at this game. Truly, it took me a few minutes before I remembered that what those men were playing was what I had been playing, against myself, during the months of my helplessness. The cipher-code which served me in my worthy exercises

was but a substitute, a symbol for these solid figures; my
astonishment that this pushing about of pieces on the
board was the same as the imaginary fantastics in my
mind, must have been like that of an astronomer who,
after complicated paper calculations as to the existence
of a new planet, eventually really sees it in the sky as a
clear, white, substantial body. I stared at the board as if
magnetized and saw there my set-up, knight, rook, king,
queen and pawns as genuine figures carved out of wood;
in order to get the hang of the game I had voluntarily to
transmute it from my abstract realm of numbers and letters into the movable figures. Gradually I was overcome
with curiosity to observe a real contest between two players. Then followed that regrettable and impolite inter-
ference of mine with your game. But that mistaken move
of your friend's was like a stab at my heart. It was pure
instinct that made me hold him back, a quite impulsive
grasp like that with which one involuntarily seizes a child
leaning over a banister. It was not until afterwards that I
became conscious of the impropriety of my intrusive-
ness."

I hastened to assure Dr. B. that we were all happy
about the incident to which we owed his acquaintance
and that, after what he had confided in me, I would be
doubly interested in the opportunity to see him at tomorrow's improvised tournament.

"Really, you mustn't expect too much. It will be nothing but a test for me—a test whether I—whether I'm at
all capable of dealing with chess in a normal way, in a
game with a real board with substantial chess-men and
a living opponent—for now I doubt more than ever that
those hundreds, they may have been thousands, of games
that I played were real games according to the rules and

not merely a sort of dream-chess, fever-chess, a delirium in which, as always in dreams, one skips intermediate steps. Surely you do not seriously believe that I would measure myself against a champion, that I expect to give tit for tat to the greatest one in the world. What interests and fascinates me is nothing but the posthumous curiosity to discover whether what went on in my cell was chess or madness, whether I was then at the dangerous brink or already beyond it—that's all, nothing else."

At this moment the gong summoning passengers to dinner was heard. The conversation must have lasted almost two hours, for Dr. B. had told me his story in much greater detail than that in which I assemble it. I thanked him warmly and took my leave. I had hardly covered the length of the deck when he was alongside me, visibly nervous, saying with something of a stutter:

"One thing more. Will you please tell your friends beforehand, so that it should not later seem discourteous, that I will play only one game. . . . The idea is merely to close an old account—a final settlement, not a new beginning. . . . I can't afford to sink back a second time into that passionate play-fever that I recall with nothing but horror. And besides—besides, the doctor warned me, expressly warned me. Every one who has ever succumbed to a mania remains for ever in jeopardy, and a sufferer from chess poisoning—even if discharged as cured—had better keep away from a chess-board. You understand, then—only this one experimental game for myself and no more."

We assembled in the smoking-room the next day promptly at the appointed hour, three o'clock. Our circle had increased by yet two more lovers of the royal game, two ship's officers who had obtained special leave from duty to watch the tourney. Czentovic, too, unlike on the preceding days, was on time, and after the usual choice of colours there began the memorable game of this *homo obscurissimus* against the celebrated master.

I regret that it was played for only us thoroughly incompetent observers and that its course is as completely lost to the annals of the art of chess as are Beethoven's improvisations to music. True, we tried to piece it together from our collective memory on the following afternoons, but vainly; very likely, in the passion of the moment, we had allowed our interest to centre on the players rather than in the game. For the intellectual contrast between the contestants became plastic physically according to their manner as the play proceeded. Czentovic, the routinier, remained as immobile as a block the entire time, his eyes unalterably fixed on the board; thinking seemed to cost him almost physical effort that called for extreme concentration on the part of every organ. Dr. B., on the other hand, was completely slack and unconstrained. Like the true dilettante, in the best sense of the word, to whom only the play in play—the *diletto*—gives joy, he relaxed fully, explained moves to us in easy conversation during the early intervals, lighted a cigarette carelessly, and glanced at the board for a minute only when it came his turn to play. Each time it seemed as if he had expected just the move that his antagonist made.

The perfunctory moves came off quite rapidly. It was not until the seventh or eighth that something like a definite plan seemed to develop. Czentovic prolonged his periods of reflection; by that we sensed that the actual battle for the lead was setting in. But to be quite frank, the gradual development of the situation represented to us lay observers, as usually in tournament games, something of a disappointment. The more the pieces wove themselves into a singular design the more impenetrable became the real lay of the land. We could not discern what one or the other rival purposed or which of the two had the advantage. We noticed merely that certain pieces insinuated themselves forward like levers to undermine the enemy front, but since every move of these superior players was part of a combination that comprised a plan for several moves ahead, we were unable to detect the strategy of their back-and-forth.

An oppressive fatigue then took possession of us, largely because of Czentovic's interminable cogitation between moves which eventually produced visible irritation in our friend, too. I observed uneasily how, the longer the game stretched out, he became increasingly restless, moving about in his chair, nervously lighting a succession of cigarettes, occasionally seizing a pencil to make a note. He would order mineral water and gulp it down, glass after glass; it was plain that his mind was working a hundred times faster than Czentovic's. Every time the latter, after endless reflection, decided to push a piece forward with his heavy hand, our friend would smile like one who encounters something long expected and make an immediate riposte. In his nimble mind he must have calculated every possibility that lay open to his opponent; the longer Czentovic took to make a decision the more his impatience grew, and during the waiting his lips narrowed into an angry and almost inimical line. Czentovic, however, did not allow himself to be hurried. He deliberated, stiff and silent, and increased the length of the pauses the more the field became de-

nuded of figures. By the forty-second move, after one and
a half hours, we sat limply by, almost indifferent to what
was going on in the arena. One of the ship's officers had
already departed, another was reading a book and would
look up only when a piece had been moved. But then
suddenly, at a move of Czentovic's, the unexpected happened. As soon as Dr. B. perceived that Czentovic took
hold of the bishop to move it, he crouched like a cat
about to spring. His whole body trembled and Czentovic
had no sooner executed his intention than he pushed his
queen forward and said loudly and triumphantly,
"There! That's done with!", fell back in his chair, his
arms crossed over his breast, and looked challengingly at
Czentovic. At once his pupils gleamed with a hot light.

Impulsively we bent over the board to figure out the
significance of the move so ostentatiously announced. At
first blush no direct threat was observable. Our friend's
statement, then, had reference to some development that
we short-thoughted amateurs could not prefigure. Czentovic was the only one among us who had not stirred at
the provocative call; he remained as still as if the insult-
ing "done with" had glanced off of him unheard. Nothing happened. Everybody held his breath and at once the
ticking of the clock that stood on the table to measure
the moves became audible. Three minutes passed, seven
minutes, eight minutes—Czentovic was motionless, but
I thought I noticed an inner tension that became manifest in the greater distention of his thick nostrils.

This silent waiting seemed to be as unbearable to our
friend as to us. He shoved his chair back, rose abruptly
and began to traverse the smoking-room, first slowly, then
quicker and quicker. Those present looked at him wonderingly, but none with greater uneasiness than I, for I

perceived that in spite of his vehemence this pacing never deviated from a uniform span; it was as if, in this awful space, he would each time come plump against an invisible cupboard that obliged him to reverse his steps. Shuddering, I recognized that it was an unconscious reproduction of the pacing in his erstwhile cell; during those months of incarceration it must have been exactly thus that he rushed to and fro, like a caged animal; his hands must have been clenched and his shoulders hunched exactly like this; it must have been like this that he pelted forward and back a thousand times there, the red lights of madness in his paralysed though feverish stare. Yet his mental control seemed still fully intact, for from time to time he turned impatiently towards the table to see if Czentovic had made up his mind. But time stretched to nine, then ten minutes.

What occurred then, at last, was something that none could have predicted. Czentovic slowly raised his heavy hand which, until then, had rested inert on the table. Tautly we all watched for the upshot. Czentovic, however, moved no piece, but rather with the back of his hand pushed, with one slow determined sweep, all the figures from the board. It took us a moment to comprehend: Czentovic gave up the game. He had capitulated in order that we might not witness his being mated. The impossible had come to pass: the champion of the world, victor at innumerable tournaments, had struck his colours before an unknown, a man who hadn't touched a chess-board for twenty or twenty-five years. Our friend, the anonymous, the ignotus, had overcome the greatest chess master on earth in open battle.

Automatically, in the excitement, one after another rose to his feet; each was animated by the feeling that he

must give vent to the joyous shock by saying or doing
something. Only one remained stolidly at rest: Czentovic. After a measured interval he lifted his head and directed a stony look at our friend.

"Another game?" he asked.

"Naturally," answered Dr. B. with an enthusiasm that
was disturbing to me, and he seated himself, even before
I could remind him of his own stipulation to play only
once, and began to set up the figures in feverish haste.
He pushed them about in such heat that a pawn twice
slid from his trembling fingers to the floor; the pained
discomfort that his unnatural excitement had already
produced in me grew to something like fear. For this
previously calm and quiet person had become visibly
exalted; the twitching of his mouth was more frequent
and in every limb he shook as with fever.

"Don't," I said softly to him. "No more now; you've
had enough for today. It's too much of a strain for you."

"Strain! Ha!" and he laughed loudly and spitefully.
"I could have played seventeen games during that slow
ride. The only strain is for me to keep awake at that
tempo.—Well, aren't you ever going to begin?"

These last words had been addressed in an impetuous,
almost rude tone to Czentovic. The latter glanced at him
quietly and evenly but there was something of a clenched
fist in that adamantine, stubborn glance. On the instant
a new element had entered: a dangerous tension, a passionate hate. No longer were they two players in a sporting way; they were two enemies sworn to destroy each
other. Czentovic hesitated long before making the first
move and I had a definite sensation that he was delaying
on purpose. No question but that this seasoned tactician
had long since discovered that just such dilatoriness

wearied and irritated his antagonist. He used no less than four minutes for the normal, the simplest of openings, moving the king's pawn two spaces. Instantly our friend advanced his king's pawn, but again Czentovic was responsible for an eternal, intolerable pause; it was like waiting with beating heart for the thunder-clap after a streak of fiery lightning, and waiting—with no thunder forthcoming. Czentovic never stirred. He meditated quietly, slowly, and as I felt increasingly, maliciously slowly—which gave me plenty of time to observe Dr. B. He had just about consumed his third glass of water; it came to my mind that he had spoken of his feverish thirst in his cell. Every symptom of abnormal excitement was plainly present: I saw his forehead grow moist and the scar on his hand become redder and more sharply outlined than before. Still, however, he held himself in rein. It was not until the fourth move when Czentovic again pondered exasperatingly that he forgot himself and exploded with, "Aren't you ever going to move?"

Czentovic looked up coldly. "As I remember it we agreed on a ten-minute limit. It is a principle with me not to make it less."

Dr. B. bit his lips. I noticed under the table the growing restlessness with which he lifted and lowered the sole of his shoe, and I could not control the nervousness that overcame me because of the oppressive prescience of some insane thing that was boiling in him. As a matter of fact, there was a second encounter at the eighth move. Dr. B., whose self-control diminished with the increasing periods of waiting, could no longer conceal his tension; he was restless in his seat and unconsciously began to drum on the table with his fingers. Again Czentovic raised his peasant head.

"May I ask you not to drum. It disturbs me. I can't play with that."

"Ha, ha," answered Dr. B. with a short laugh, "one can see that."

Czentovic flushed. "What do you mean by that?" he asked, sharply and evilly.

Dr. B. gave another curt and spiteful laugh. "Nothing except that it's plain that you're nervous."

Czentovic lowered his head and said nothing. Seven minutes elapsed before he made his move, and that was the funereal tempo at which the game dragged on. Czentovic became correspondingly stonier; in the end he utilized the maximum time before determining on a move, and from interval to interval the conduct of our friend became stranger and stranger. It looked as if he no longer had any interest in the game but was occupied with something quite different. He abandoned his excited pacing and remained seated motionlessly. Staring into the void with a vacant and almost insane look, he uninterruptedly muttered unintelligible words; either he was absorbed in endless combinations or—and this was my inner suspicion—he was working out quite other games, for each time that Czentovic got around to making a move he had to be recalled from his absent state. Then it took a minute or two to orient himself. My conviction grew that he had really forgotten all about Czentovic and the rest of us in this cold aspect of his insanity which might at any instant discharge itself violently. Surely enough, at the nineteenth move the crisis came. No sooner had Czentovic executed his play than Dr. B., giving no more than a cursory look at the board, suddenly pushed his bishop three spaces forward and shouted so loudly that we all started:

"Check! Check, the king!"

Every eye was on the board in anticipation of an ex-traordinary move. Then, after a minute, there was an unexpected development. Very slowly Czentovic tilted his head and looked—which he had never done before —from one face to another. Something seemed to afford him a rich enjoyment, for little by little his lips gave expression to a satisfied and scornful smile. Only after he had savoured to the full the triumph which was still unintelligible to us did he address us, saying with mock deference:

"Sorry—but I see no check. Perhaps one of you gen-tlemen can see my king in check?"

We looked at the board and then uneasily over at Dr. B. Czentovic's king was fully covered against the bishop by a pawn—a child could see that—thus the king could not possibly be in check. We turned one to the other. Might not our friend in his agitation have pushed a piece over the line, a square too far one way or the other? His at-tention arrested by our silence, Dr. B. now stared at the board and began, stutteringly:

"But the king ought to be on f7—that's wrong, all wrong— Your move was wrong! All the pieces are mis-placed—the pawn belongs on g5 and not on g4. Why, that's quite a different game—that's—"

He halted abruptly. I had seized his arm roughly, or rather I had pinched it so hard that even in his feverish bewilderment he could not but feel my grip. He turned and looked at me like a somnambulist.

"What—what do you want?"

I only said "Remember!" at the same time lightly drawing my finger over the scar on his hand. Automat-ically he followed my gesture, his eyes fixed glassily on the blood-red streak. Suddenly he began to tremble and his body shook.

"For God's sake," he whispered with pale lips. "Have I said or done something silly? Is it possible that I'm again . . . ?"

"No," I said, in a low voice, "but you have to stop the game at once. It's high time. Recollect what the doctor said."

With a single movement Dr. B. was on his feet. "I have to apologize for my stupid mistake," he said in his old, polite voice, inclining himself to Czentovic. "What I said was plain nonsense, of course. It goes without saying that the game is yours." Then to us: "My apologies to you gentlemen, also. But I warned you beforehand not to expect too much from me. Forgive the disgrace—it is the last time that I yield to the temptation of chess."

He bowed and left in the same modest and mysterious manner in which he had first appeared before us. I alone knew why this man would never again touch a chessboard, while the others, a bit confused, stood around with that vague feeling of having narrowly escaped something uncomfortable and dangerous. "Damned fool," MacIver grumbled in his disappointment.

Last of all, Czentovic rose from his chair, half glancing at the unfinished game.

"Too bad," he said generously. "The attack wasn't at all badly conceived. The man certainly has lots of talent for an amateur."

AMOK

In March, 1912, when a big mail-boat was unloading at Naples, there was an accident about which extremely inaccurate reports appeared in the newspapers. I myself saw nothing of the affair, for (in common with many of the passengers), wishing to escape the noise and discomfort of coaling, I had gone to spend the evening ashore. As it happens, however, I am in a position to know what really occurred, and to explain the cause. So many years have now elapsed since the incidents about to be related, that there is no reason why I should not break the silence I have hitherto maintained.

I had been travelling in the Federated Malay States. Recalled home by cable on urgent private affairs, I joined the *Wotan* at Singapore, and had to put up with very poor accommodation. My cabin was a hole of a place squeezed into a corner close to the engine-room, small, hot, and dark. The fusty, stagnant air reeked of oil. I had to keep the electric fan running, with the result that a fetid draught crawled over my face reminding me of the fluttering of a crazy bat. From beneath came the persistent rattle and groans of the engines, which sounded like a coal-porter tramping and wheezing as he climbed an unending flight of iron stairs; from above came the no less persistent tread of feet upon the promenade deck. As soon as I had had my cabin baggage properly stowed away, I fled from the place to the upper deck, where with delight I inhaled deep breaths of the balmy south wind.

But on this crowded ship the promenade deck, too, was full of bustle and disquiet. It was thronged with passengers, nervously irritable in their enforced idleness and unavoidable proximity, chattering without pause as they prowled to and fro. The light laughter of the women who reclined in deck-chairs, the twists and turns of those who were taking a constitutional on the encumbered deck, the general hubbub, were uncongenial. In Malaysia, and before that in Burma and Siam, I had been visiting an unfamiliar world. My mind was filled with new impressions, with lively images which chased one another in rapid succession. I wanted to contemplate them at leisure, to sort and arrange them, to digest and assimilate; but in this noisy boulevard, humming with life of a very different kind, there was no chance of finding the necessary repose. If I tried to read, the lines in the printed page ran together before my tired eyes when the shadows of the passers-by flickered over the white page. I could never be alone with myself and my thoughts in this thickly peopled alley.

For three days I did my utmost to possess my soul in patience, resigned to my fellow-passengers, staring at the sea. The sea was always the same, blue and void, except that at nightfall for a brief space it became resplendent with a play of varied colours. As for the people, I had grown sick of their faces before the three days were up. I knew every detail of them all. I was surfeited with them, and equally surfeited with the giggling of the women and with the windy argumentativeness of some Dutch officers coming home on leave. I took refuge in the saloon; though from this haven, too, I was speedily driven away because a group of English girls from Shanghai spent their time between meals hammering out waltzes on the piano. There was nothing for it but my cabin. I turned in after luncheon, having drugged myself with a couple of bottles of beer, resolved to escape dinner and the dance that was to follow, hoping to sleep the clock round and more, and thus to spend the better part of a day in oblivion.

When I awoke it was dark, and stuffier than ever in the little coffin. I had switched off the fan, and was dripping with sweat. I felt heavy after my prolonged slumber, and some minutes slipped by before I fully realized where I was. It must certainly be past midnight, for there was no music to be heard, and the tramp-tramp of feet overhead had ceased. The only sound was that of the machinery, the beating heart of the leviathan, who wheezed and groaned as he bore his living freight onward through the darkness.

I groped my way to the deck, where there was not a soul to be seen. Looking first at the smoking funnels and the ghostlike spars, I then turned my eyes upward and saw that the sky was clear; dark velvet, sprinkled with stars. It looked as if a curtain had been drawn across a vast source of light, and as if the stars were tiny rents in the curtain, through which that indescribable radiance poured. Never had I seen such a sky.

The night was refreshingly cool, as so often at this hour on a moving ship even at the equator. I breathed the fragrant air, charged with the aroma of distant isles. For the first time since I had come on board I was seized with a longing to dream, conjoined with another desire, more sensuous, to surrender my body—womanlike—to the night's soft embrace. I wanted to lie down some-

where, and gaze at the white hieroglyphs in the starry
expanse. But the long chairs were all stacked and inaccessible. Nowhere on the empty deck was there a place
for a dreamer to rest.

I made for the forecastle, stumbling over ropes and
past iron windlasses to the bow, where I leaned over the
rail watching the stem as it rose and fell, rhythmically,
cutting its way through the phosphorescent waters. Did
I stand there for an hour, or only for a few minutes?
Who can tell? Rocked in that giant cradle, I took no
note of the passing of time. All I was conscious of was
a gentle lassitude, which was wellnigh voluptuous. I
wanted to sleep, to dream; yet I was loath to quit this
wizard's world, to return to my 'tween-decks coffin. Moving a pace or two, I felt with one foot a coil of rope. I
sat down, and, closing my eyes, abandoned myself to
the drowsy intoxication of the night. Soon the fron-
tiers of consciousness became obscured; I was not sure
whether the sound I heard was that of my own breathing or that of the mechanical heart of the ship; I gave
myself up more and more completely, more and more
passively, to the environing charm of this midnight
world.

A dry cough near at hand recalled me to my senses
with a start. Opening eyes that were now attuned to the
darkness, I saw close beside me the faint gleam of a pair
of spectacles, and a few inches below this a fitful glow
which obviously came from a pipe. Before I sat down
I had been intent on the stars and the sea, and had thus
overlooked this neighbour, who must have been sitting
here motionless all the while. Still a little hazy as to
my whereabouts, but feeling as if somehow I was an

intruder, I murmured apologetically in my native German: "Excuse me!" The answer came promptly, "Not at all!" in the same language, and with an unmistakably German intonation.

It was strange and eerie, this darkling juxtaposition to an unseen and unknown person. I had the sensation that he was staring vainly at me just as I was staring vainly at him. Neither of us could see more than a dim silhouette, black against a dusky background. I could just hear his breathing and the faint gurgle of his pipe.

The silence became unbearable. I should have liked to get up and go away, but was restrained by the conviction that to do this without a word would be unpardonably rude. In my embarrassment I took out a cigarette and struck a match. For a second or two there was light, and we could see one another. What I saw was the face of a stranger, a man I had never yet seen in the dining saloon or on the promenade deck; a face which (was it only because the lineaments were caricatured in that momentary illumination?) seemed extraordinarily sinister and suggestive of a hobgoblin. Before I had been able to note details accurately, the darkness closed in again, so that once more all that was visible was the fitful glow from the pipe, and above it the occasional glint of the glasses. Neither of us spoke. The silence was sultry and oppressive, like tropical heat.

At length I could bear it no longer. Standing up, I said a civil "Good night."

"Good night!" came the answer, in a harsh and raucous voice.

As I stumbled aft amid the encumbrances on the foredeck, I heard footsteps behind me, hasty and uncertain. My neighbour on the coil of rope was following me with

unsteady gait. He did not come quite close, but through
the darkness I could sense his anxiety and uneasiness.

He was speaking hurriedly.

"You'll forgive me if I ask you a favour. I . . . I,"
he hesitated, "I . . . I have private, extremely private
reasons for keeping to myself on board. . . . In mourning. . . . That's why I have made no acquaintances
during the voyage. You excepted, of course. . . . What
I want is . . . I mean I should be very greatly obliged
if you would refrain from telling any one that you have
seen me here. It is, let me repeat, strictly private grounds
that prevent my joining in the life of the ship, and it
would be most distressing to me were you to let fall
a word about my frequenting this forecastle alone at
night. I . . ."

He paused, and I was prompt in assuring him that
his wishes should be respected. I was but a casual trav-
eller, I said, and had no friends on board. We shook
hands. I went back to my cabin to sleep out the night.
But my slumbers were uneasy, for I had troublous
dreams.

I kept my promise to say nothing to any one about
my strange encounter, though the temptation to indiscretion was considerable. On a sea voyage the veriest
trifle is an event—a sail on the horizon, a shoal of por-
poises, a new flirtation, a practical joke. Besides, I was
full of curiosity about this remarkable fellow-passenger.
I scanned the list of bookings in search of a name which
might fit him; and I looked at this person and that, wondering if they knew anything about him. All day I suffered from nervous impatience, waiting for nightfall
when I hoped I might meet him again. Psychological

enigmas have invariably fascinated me. An encounter
with an inscrutable character makes me thrill with longing to pluck the heart out of the mystery, the urge of
this desire being hardly less vehement than that of a
man's desire to possess a woman. The day seemed in-
sufferably long. I went to bed early, certain that an in-
ternal alarum would awaken me in the small hours.

Thus it was. I awoke at about the same time as on
the previous night. Looking at my watch, whose figures
and hands stood out luminous from the dial, I saw that
the hour had just gone two. Quickly I made for the
deck.

In the tropics the weather is less changeable than in
our northern climes. The night was as before: dark,
clear, and lit with brilliant stars. But in myself there
was a difference. I no longer felt dreamy and easeful,
was no longer agreeably lulled by the gentle swaying of
the ship. An intangible something confused and disturbed me, drew me irresistibly to the fore-deck. I
wanted to know whether the mysterious stranger would
again be sitting there, solitary, on the coil of rope. Re-
luctant and yet eager, I yielded to the impulse. As I
neared the place, I caught sight of what looked like a
red and glowing eye—his pipe. He was there!

Involuntarily I stopped short, and was about to retreat, when the dark figure rose, took two steps forward,
and, coming close to me, said in an apologetic and life-
less voice:

"Sorry! I'm sure you were coming back to your old
place, and it seems to me that you were about to turn
away because you saw me. Won't you sit down? I'm
just off."

I hastened to rejoin that I was only on the point of withdrawing because I was afraid of disturbing him, and that I hoped he would stay.

"You won't disturb me!" he said with some bitterness. "Far from it; I am glad not to be alone once in a while. For days upon days I have hardly spoken to a soul; years, it seems; and I find it almost more than I can bear to have to bottle everything up in myself. I can't sit in the cabin any longer, the place is like a prison-cell; and yet I can't stand the passengers either, for they chatter and laugh all day. Their perpetual frivolling drives me frantic. The silly noise they make finds its way into my cabin, so that I have to stop my ears. Of course, they don't know I can hear them, or how they exasperate me. Not that they'd care if they did, for they're only a pack of foreigners."

He suddenly pulled himself up, saying: "But I know I must be boring you. I didn't mean to be so loquacious."

He bowed, and moved to depart, but I pressed him to stay.

"You are not boring me in the least. Far from it, for I too am glad to have a quiet talk up here under the stars. Won't you have a cigarette?"

As he lighted it, I again got a glimpse of his face, the face which was now that of an acquaintance. In the momentary glare, before he threw away the match, he looked earnestly, searchingly at me, appealingly it almost seemed, as his spectacled eyes fixed themselves on mine.

I felt a thrill akin to horror. This man, so it seemed to me, had a tale to tell, was on fire to tell it, but some inward hindrance held him back. Only by silence, a si-

lence that invited confidence, could I help him to throw
off his restraint.

We sat down on the coil of rope, half facing one another, leaning against the top rail. His nervousness was
betrayed by the shaking of the hand which held the cigarette. We smoked, and still I said never a word. At
length he broke the silence.

"Are you tired?"

"Not an atom!"

"I should rather like to ask you something." He hesitated. "It would be more straightforward to say I want
to tell you something. I know how ridiculous it is of
me to begin babbling like this to the first comer; but,
mentally speaking, I'm in a tight place. I've got to the
point where I simply must tell some one, or else go
clean off my head. You'll understand why, as soon as
I've told you. Of course, you can do nothing to help me,
but keeping my trouble to myself is making me very
ill, and you know what fools sick folk are—or what fools
they seem to healthy people."

I interrupted him, and begged him not to distress
himself with fancies of that sort, but to go ahead with
his story. "Naturally there would be no meaning in my
giving you unlimited promises of help, when I don't
know the situation. Still, I can at least assure you of my
willingness to give you what help I may. That's one's
plain duty, isn't it, to show that one's ready to pull a
fellow-mortal out of a hole? One can try to help, at
least."

"Duty to offer help? Duty to try, at least? Duty to
show that one's ready to pull a fellow-mortal out of a
hole?"

Thus did he repeat what I had said, staccato, in a

tone of unwonted bitterness flavoured with mockery, whose significance was to become plain to me later. For the moment, there was something in his scanning iteration of my words which made me wonder whether he was mad, or drunk.

As if guessing my thoughts, he went on in a more ordinary voice: "You'll perhaps think me queer in the head, or that I've been imbibing too freely in my loneliness. That's not what's the matter, and I'm sane enough—so far! What set me off was one word you used, and the connexion in which you happened to use it, the word 'duty.' It touched me on the raw, and I'm raw all over, for the strange thing is that what torments me all the time is a question of duty, duty, duty."

He pulled himself up with a jerk. Without further circumlocution, he began to explain himself clearly.

"I'm a doctor, you must know. That's a vital point in my story. Now in medical practice one often has to deal with cases in which duty is not so plain as you might think. Fateful cases; you can call them borderline cases, if you like. In these cases there's not just one obvious duty; there are conflicting duties: one duty of the ordinary kind, which runs counter to a duty to the State, and perhaps on the other side runs counter to a duty to science. Help pull a fellow-mortal out of a hole? Of course one should. That's what one's there for. But such maxims are purely theoretical. In a practical instance, how far is help to go? Here you turn up, a nocturnal visitant, and, though you've never seen me before, and I've no claim on you, I ask you not to tell any one you've seen me. Well, you hold your tongue, because you feel it your duty to help me in the way I ask. Then you turn up again, and I beg you to let me talk to you because silence is eating my heart out. You are good enough to listen. After all, that's easy enough. I haven't asked you anything very difficult. But suppose I were to say: 'Catch hold of me and throw me overboard!' You would quickly reach the limit of your complaisance, wouldn't you? You would no longer regard it as a 'duty to help,' I suppose! There must be a limit somewhere. This duty of which you speak, surely it comes to an end before the point is reached at which one's own life is gravely imperilled, or one's own responsibility to accepted public institutions is affected? Or perhaps this duty to help has no limits at all, where a doctor is concerned? Should a doctor be a universal saviour, simply because he has a diploma couched in Latin? Has he for that reason to fling away his life when some one happens along and implores him to be helpful and kindhearted? There is a limit to one's duty, and one reaches it when one is at the end of one's tether!"

He went off at a tangent once more.

"I'm sorry to show so much excitement. It's not because I'm drunk. I'm not drunk—yet. True, I'm drinking heavily here on board; and I've got drunk now and again of late, for my life has been so damnably lonely in the East. Just think, for seven years I've been living almost exclusively among natives and animals; and in such conditions one naturally forgets how to talk sanely and calmly. When, at last, one gets a chance of talking to a man of one's own people, one's tongue runs away with one. Where was I? I was going to put a question to you, was going to place a problem before you, to ask you whether it was really incumbent on one to help, no matter in what circumstances, as an angel from heaven might help. . . . But I'm afraid it will be rather a long business. You're really not tired?"

"Not the least bit in the world!"

He was groping behind him in the darkness. I heard something clink, and could make out the forms of a couple of bottles. He poured from one of them into a glass, and handed it to me—a large peg of neat whiskey.

"Won't you have a drink?"

To keep him company, I sipped, while he, for lack of another glass, took a bountiful swig from the bottle. There was a moment's silence, during which came five strokes on the ship's bell. It was half-past two in the morning.

"Well, I want to put a case before you. Suppose there was a doctor practising in a little town—in the country, really. A doctor who . . ."

He broke off, hesitated a while, and then made a fresh start.

"No, that won't do. I must tell you the whole thing exactly as it happened, and as it happened to myself. A direct narrative from first to last. Otherwise you'll never be able to understand. There must be no false shame, no concealment. When people come to consult me, they have to strip to the buff, have to show me their excreta. If I am to help them, they must make no bones about informing me as to the most private matters. It will be of no use for me to tell you of something that happened to some one else, to a mythical Doctor Somebody, somewhere and somewhen. I shall strip naked, as if I were your patient. Anyway, I have forgotten all decency in that horrible place where I have been living, in that hideous solitude, in a land which eats the soul out of one's body and sucks the marrow out of one's bones."

I must have made some slight movement of protest, for he went off on a side issue.

"Ah, I can see you are an enthusiast for the East, an admirer of the temples and the palm trees, filled full with the romance of the regions where you have been travelling for your pleasure, to while away a month or two. No doubt the tropics are charming to one who hurries or saunters through them by rail, in a motor car, or in a rickshaw. I felt the same when I first came out here seven years ago. I was full of dreams about what I was going to do: learn the native tongue; read the Sacred Books in the original; study tropical diseases; do original scientific work; master the psychology of the indigenes (thus do we phrase it in our European jargon); become a missionary of civilization. . . .

"But life out there is like living in a hothouse with invisible walls. It saps the energies. You get fever, though you swallow quinine by the teaspoonful; and fever takes all the guts out of you, you become limp and lazy, as soft as a jellyfish. A European is cut adrift from his moorings if he has to leave the big towns and is sent to one of those accursed settlements in a jungle or a swamp. Sooner or later he will lose his poise. Some take to drink; others learn opium-smoking from the Chinese; others find relief in brutality, sadism, or what not—they all go off the rails. How one longs for home! To walk along a street with proper buildings in it! To sit in a solidly constructed room with glass windows, and among white men and women. So it goes on year after year, until at length the time for home leave comes round—and a man

finds he has grown too inert even to take his furlough.
What would be the use? He knows he has been forgotten, and that if he did go home there would be no wel-
come awaiting him or, worse still, his coming might be
utterly ignored. So he stays where he is, in a mangrove
swamp, or in a steaming forest. It was a sad day for me
when I sold myself into servitude on the equator.

"Besides, forgoing my home leave was not quite so
voluntary an affair as I have implied. I had studied medicine in Germany, where I was born, and, soon after I
was qualified, I got a good post at the Leipzig Clinic.
If you were to look up the files of the medical papers of
that date, you would find that a new method of treatment I advocated for one of the commoner diseases made
some little stir, so that I had been a good deal talked
about for so young a man.

"Then came a love affair which ruined my chances.
It was with a woman whose acquaintance I made at the
hospital. She'd been living with a man she'd driven so
crazy that he tried to shoot himself and failed to make
a clean job of it. Soon I was as crazy as he. She had a
sort of cold pride about her which I found irresistible.
Women that are domineering and rather impudent can
always do anything they like with me, but this woman
reduced me to pulp. I did whatever she wanted and in
the end (it seems hard to tell you, though the story's an
old one now, dating from eight years ago) for her sake
I stole some money from the hospital safe. The thing
came out, of course, and there was the devil to pay. An
uncle of mine made the loss good, but there was no more
career for me in Leipzig.

"Just at this time I heard that the Dutch Government was short of doctors in the colonial service, would

take Germans, and was actually offering a premium. That told me there must be a catch in it somewhere, and I knew well enough that in these tropical plantations tombstones grow as luxuriantly as the vegetation. But when one is young one is always ready to believe that fever and death will strike some other fellow down and give one's self the go-by.

"After all, I hadn't much choice. I made my way to Rotterdam, signed on for ten years, and got a fine, thick wad of banknotes. I sent half of them to my uncle. A girl of the town got the rest—the half of the premium and any other money I could raise—all because she was so like the young woman to whom I owed my downfall. Without money, without even a watch, without illusions, I steamed away from Europe, and was by no means sad at heart when the vessel cleared the port. I sat on deck much as you are sitting now; ready to take delight in the East, in the palm trees under new skies; dreaming of the wonderful forests, of solitude, and of peace.

"I soon had my fill of solitude. They did not station me in Batavia or in Surabaya, in one of the big towns where there are human beings with white skins, a club and a golf-course, books and newspapers. They sent me to—well, never mind the name! A god-forgotten place up country, a day's journey from the nearest town. The 'society' consisted of two or three dull-witted and sun-dried officials and one or two half-castes. The settlement was encircled by interminable forests, plantations, jungles, and swamps.

"Still, it was tolerable at first. There was the charm of novelty. I studied hard for a time. Then the Vice-Resident was making a tour of inspection through the

district, and had a motor smash. Compound fracture
of the leg, no other doctor within hail, an operation
needed, followed by a good recovery—and a considerable amount of kudos for me, since the patient was a
big gun. I did some anthropological work, on the poi-
sons and weapons used by the primitives. Until the
freshness had worn off, I found a hundred and one
things which helped to keep me alive.

"This lasted just as long as the vigour I had brought
with me from Europe. Then the climate got hold of
me. The other white men in the settlement bored me to
death. I shunned their company, began to drink rather
heavily, and to browse on my own weary thoughts. After
all, I had only to stick it for another two years. Then
I could retire on a pension, and start life afresh in Europe. Nothing to do but wait till the time was up. And
there I should still be waiting, but for the unexpected
happening I am going to tell you about."

The voice in the darkness ceased. So still was the night
that once more I could hear the sound of the ship's stem
clearing the water, and the distant pulsing of the machinery. I should have been glad to light a cigarette, but
I was afraid I might startle the narrator by any sudden
movement and by the unexpected glare.

For a time the silence was unbroken. Had he changed
his mind, and decided it would be indiscreet to tell me
any more? Had he dropped off into a doze?

While I was thus meditating, six bells struck. It was
three in the morning. He stirred, and I heard a faint
clink as he picked up the whiskey bottle. He was prim-
ing himself again. Then he resumed, with a fresh access
of tense passion.

"Well, so things went with me. Month after month, I had been sitting inactive in that detestable spot, as motionless as a spider in the centre of its web. The rainy season was over. For weeks I had been listening to the downpour on the roof, and not a soul had come near me—no European, that is to say. I had been alone in the house with my native servants and my whiskey. Being even more homesick than usual, when I read in a novel about lighted streets and white women, my fingers would begin to tremble. You are only what we call a globe-trotter; you don't know the country as those who live there know it. A white man is seized at times by what might be accounted one of the tropical diseases, a nostalgia so acute as to drive him almost into delirium. Well, in some such paroxysm I was poring over an atlas, dreaming of journeys possible and impossible. At this moment two of my servants came, open-mouthed with astonishment, to say that a lady had called to see me— a white lady.

"I, too, was amazed. I had heard no sound of carriage or of car. What the devil was a white woman doing in this wilderness?

"I was sitting in the upstairs veranda of my two-storied house, and not dressed for white company. In the minute or two that were needed for me to make myself presentable, I was able to pull myself together a little; but I was still nervous, uneasy, filled with disagreeable forebodings, when at length I went downstairs. Who on earth could it be? I was friendless. Why should a white woman come to visit me in the wilds?

"The lady was sitting in the ante-room, and behind her chair was standing a China boy, obviously her servant. As she jumped up to greet me, I saw that her face was hidden by a thick motor-veil. She began to speak before I could say a word.

" 'Good morning, Doctor,' she said in English. 'You'll excuse my dropping in like this without an appointment, won't you?' She spoke rather rapidly, almost as if repeating a speech which had been mentally rehearsed. 'When we were driving through the settlement, and had to stop the car for a moment, I remembered that you lived here.' This was puzzling! If she had come in a car, why hadn't she driven up to the house? 'I've heard so much about you—what a wonder you worked when the Vice-Resident had that accident. I saw him the other day playing golf as well as ever. Your name is in every one's mouth down there, and we'd all gladly give away our grumpy old senior surgeon and his two assistants if we could but get you in exchange. Besides, why do you never come to headquarters? You live up here like a yogi!'

"She ran on and on, without giving me a chance to get in a word edgewise. Manifestly her loquacity was the outcome of nervousness, and it made me nervous in my turn. 'Why does she go on chattering like this?' I wondered. 'Why doesn't she tell me who she is? Why doesn't she take off her veil? Has she got fever? Is she a madwoman?' I grew more and more distrait, feeling like a fool as I stood there mumchance, while she overwhelmed me with her babble. At length the stream ran dry, so that I was able to invite her upstairs. She made a sign to the boy to stay where he was, and swept up the stairway in front of me.

" 'Pleasant quarters here,' she exclaimed, letting her gaze roam over my sitting-room. 'Ah, what lovely books. How I should like to read them all!' She strolled to the bookcase and began to con the titles. For the first time

since she had said good morning to me, she was silent for
a space.

" 'May I offer you a cup of tea?' I inquired.

"She answered without turning round.

" 'No, thank you, Doctor. I've only a few minutes to
spare. Hullo, there's Flaubert's *Éducation sentimentale*.
What a book! So you read French, too. Wonderful people, you Germans—they teach you so many languages at
school. It must be splendid to be able to speak them as
you do. The Vice-Resident swears he would never allow
any one but you to use a knife on him. That senior surgeon of ours, all he's fit for is bridge. But you—well, it
came into my head today that I should like to consult
you, and, as I was driving through the settlement, I
thought to myself, "There's no time like the present!"
But'—all this she said without looking at me, for she kept
her face towards the books—'I expect you're frightfully
busy. Perhaps I'd better call another day?'

" 'Are you going to show your cards at last?' I wondered. Of course I gave no sign of this, but assured her
that I was at her service, now or later, as she preferred.

" 'Oh, well, since I'm here!' she turned half round
towards me, but did not look up, continuing to flutter
the pages of a book she had taken from the shelf. 'It's
nothing serious. The sort of troubles women often have.
Giddiness, fainting-fits, nausea. This morning in the car,
when we were rounding a curve, I suddenly lost my senses
completely. The boy had to hold me up, or I should have
slipped on to the floor. He got me some water, and then
I felt better. I suppose the chauffeur must have been driving too fast. Don't you think so, Doctor?'

" 'I can't answer that offhand. Have you had many such
fainting-fits?'

" 'No. Not until recently, that is. During the last few weeks, pretty often. And I've been feeling so sick in the mornings.'

"She was back at the bookcase, had taken down another volume, and was fluttering the pages as before. Why did she behave so strangely? Why didn't she lift her veil and look me in the face? Purposely I made no answer. It pleased me to let her wait. If she could behave queerly, so could I! At length she went on, in her nonchalant, detached way:

" 'You agree, don't you, Doctor? It can't be anything serious. Not one of those horrid tropical diseases, surely? Nothing dangerous.'

" 'I must see if you have any fever. Let me feel your pulse.'

"I moved towards her, but she evaded me.

" 'No, Doctor, I'm sure I have no fever. I've taken my temperature every day since . . . since I began to be troubled with this faintness. Never above normal. And my digestion's all right, too.'

"I hesitated for a little. The visitor's strange manner had aroused my suspicions. Obviously she wanted to get something out of me. She had not driven a couple of hundred miles into this remote corner in order to discuss Flaubert! I kept her waiting for a minute or two before saying: 'Excuse me, but may I ask you a few plain questions?'

" 'Of course, of course. One comes to a doctor for that,' she said lightly. But she had turned her back on me again, and was fiddling with the books.

" 'Have you had any children?'

" 'Yes, one, a boy.'

" 'Well, did you have the same sort of symptoms then, in the early months, when you were pregnant?'

" 'Yes.'

"The answer was decisive, blunt, and no longer in the tone of mere prattle which had characterized her previous utterances.

" 'Well, isn't it possible that that's what's the matter with you now?'

" 'Yes.'

"Again the response was sharp and decisive.

" 'You'd better come into my consulting-room. An examination will settle the question in a moment.'

"At length she turned to face me squarely, and I could almost feel her eyes piercing me through her veil.

" 'No need for that, Doctor. I haven't a shadow of doubt as to my condition.' "

A pause.

I heard the narrator take another dose of his favourite stimulant. Then he resumed.

"Think the matter over for yourself. I had been rotting away there in my loneliness, and then this woman turned up from nowhere, the first white woman I had seen for years—and I felt as if something evil, something dangerous, had come into my room. Her iron determination made my flesh creep. She had come, it seemed, for idle chatter; and then without warning she voiced a demand as if she were throwing a knife at me. For what she wanted of me was plain enough. That was not the first time women had come to me with such a request. But they had come imploringly, had with tears besought me to help them in their trouble. Here, however, was a woman of exceptional, of virile determination. From the outset I had felt that she was stronger than I, that she could probably mould me to her will. Yet if there were evil in the room, it was in me likewise, in me the man. Bitterness had risen in me, a revolt against her. I had sensed in her an enemy.

"For a time I maintained an obstinate silence. I felt that she was eyeing me from behind her veil, that she was challenging me; that she wanted to force me to speak. But I was not ready to comply. When I did answer, I spoke beside the point, as if unconsciously mimicking her discursive and indifferent manner. I pretended that I had not understood her; tried to compel her to be candid. I was unwilling to meet her half way. I wanted her to implore me, as the others had done—wanted it for the very reason that she had approached me so imperiously, and precisely because I knew myself to be a weakling in face of such arrogance as hers.

"Consequently, I talked all round the subject, saying that her symptoms were of trifling importance, that such fainting-fits were common form in early pregnancy, and that, far from being ominous, they generally meant that things would go well. I quoted cases I had seen and cases I had read of; I treated the whole affair as a bagatelle; I talked and talked, waiting for her to interrupt me. For I knew she would have to cut me short.

"She did so with a wave of the hand, as if sweeping my words of reassurance into the void.

" 'That's not what worries me, Doctor. I'm not so well as I was the time before. My heart troubles me.'

" 'Heart trouble, you say?' I rejoined, feigning an anxiety I did not feel. 'Well, I'd better go into that at once.' I made a movement as if to reach for my stethoscope.

"Once more she was recalcitrant. She spoke commandingly, almost like a drill-sergeant.

" 'You may take my word for it that I have heart trouble. I don't want to waste my time and yours with examinations that are quite unnecessary. Besides, I think you might show a little more confidence in what I tell you. I have trusted you to the full!'

"This was a declaration of war. She had thrown down the glove, and I did not hesitate to lift it.

" 'Trust implies frankness, perfect frankness. Please speak to me straightforwardly. But, above all, take off your veil and sit down. Let the books alone and put your cards on the table. One doesn't keep a veil on when one comes to consult a medical man.'

"In her turn she accepted the challenge. Sitting down in front of me, she lifted her veil. The face thus disclosed was the sort of face I had dreaded; it was controlled and inscrutable; one of those exceptionally beautiful English faces which age cannot wither; but this lovely woman was still quite young, this woman with grey eyes that seemed so full of self-confident repose, and yet to hint at depths of passion. Her lips were firmly set, and would betray nothing she wished to keep to herself. For a full minute we gazed at one another; she imperiously and yet questioningly, with a look almost cruelly cold, so that in the end I had to lower my eyes.

"Her knuckles rattled against the table. She could not shake off her nervousness. Suddenly she said:

" 'Doctor, do you or do you not know what I want of you?'

" 'I can make a shrewd guess, I fancy! Let us speak plainly. You want to put an end to your present condition. You want me to free you from the fainting-fits, the nausea, and so on—by removing the cause. Is that it?'

" 'Yes.'

"The word was as decisive as the fall of the knife in a guillotine.

" 'Are you aware that such things are dangerous—to both the persons concerned?'

" 'Yes.'

" 'That the operation is illegal?'

" 'I know that there are circumstances in which it is not prohibited; nay, in which it is regarded as essential.'

" 'Yes, when there are good medical grounds for under- taking it.'

" 'Well, you can find such grounds. You are a doctor.'

"She looked at me without a quiver, as if issuing an order; and I, the weakling, trembled in my amazement at the elemental power of her resolve. Yet I still resisted. I would not let her see that she was too strong for me. 'Not so fast,' I thought. 'Make difficulties! Compel her to sue!'

" 'A doctor cannot always find sufficient reasons. Still, I don't mind having a consultation with one of my col- leagues. . . .'

" 'I don't want one of your colleagues. It is you I have come to consult.'

" 'Why me, may I ask?'

"She regarded me coldly, and said:

" 'I don't mind telling you that! I came to you because you live in an out-of-the-way place, because you have never met me before, because of your known ability, and because' . . . she hesitated for the first time, 'because . . . you are not likely to stay in Java much longer— especially if you have a large sum of money in hand to go home with.'

"A shiver ran through me. This mercantile calculation made my flesh creep. No tears, no beseeching. She had taken my measure, had reckoned up my price, and had sought me out in full confidence that she could mould me to her will. In truth, I was almost overpowered; but her attitude towards me filled me with gall, and I constrained myself to reply with a chilly, almost sarcastic inflexion:

" 'This large sum of money you speak of, you offer it me for . . . ?'

" 'For your help now, to be followed by your immediate departure from the Dutch Indies.'

" 'Surely you must know that that would cost me my pension?'

" 'The fee I propose would more than compensate you.'

" 'You are good enough to use plain terms, but I should like you to be even more explicit. What fee were you thinking of?'

" 'One hundred thousand gulden, in a draft on Amsterdam.'

"I trembled, both with anger and surprise. She had reckoned it all out, had calculated my price, and offered me this preposterous fee upon the condition that I should break my contract with the Dutch Government; she had bought me before seeing me; she had counted on my compliance. I felt like slapping her face, so angered was I by this contumelious treatment. But when I rose up in my wrath (she, too, was standing once more), the sight of that proud, cold mouth of hers which would not beg a favour, the flash of her arrogant eyes, aroused the brute in me, and of a sudden I burned with desire. Something in my expression must have betrayed my feeling, for she raised her eyebrows as one does when a beggar is importunate. In that instant we hated one another, and were aware of our mutual detestation. She hated me because she had to make use of me, and I hated her because she demanded, my help instead of imploring it. In this moment of silence we were for the first time speaking frankly to one another. As if a venomous serpent had bitten me, a terrible thought entered my mind, and I said to her . . . I said to her . . .

"But I go too fast, and you will misunderstand me. I must first of all explain to you whence this crazy notion came."

He paused. More whiskey. His voice was stronger when he resumed.

"I'm not trying to make excuses for myself. But I don't want you to misunderstand me. I suppose I've never been what is called a 'good' man, and yet I think I've always been ready to help people whenever I could. In the rotten sort of life I had to live out there, my one pleasure was to use the knowledge I had scraped together, and thus to give poor sick wretches new hopes of health. That's a creative pleasure, you know; makes a man feel as if, for once, he were a god. It was pure delight to me when a brown-skinned Javanese was brought in, foot swollen to the size of his head from snake-bite, shrieking with terror lest the only thing that would save him might be an amputation—and I was able to save both life and leg. I have driven hours into the jungle to help a native woman laid up with fever. At Leipzig, in the clinic, I was ready enough, sometimes, to help women in just the same plight as my lady here. But in those cases, at least, one felt that one's patient had come to one in bitter need, asking to be rescued from death or from despair. It was the feeling of another's need that made me ready to help.

"But this particular woman—how can I make you understand? She had irritated me from the first moment when she dropped in with the pretence that she was on a casual excursion. Her arrogance had set my back up. Her manner had aroused the slumbering demon, the Caliban that lies hidden in us all. I was furious that she should come to me with her fine-lady airs, with her assumption of dispassionateness in what was really a life-or-death matter. Besides, a woman does not get in the family way from playing golf, or some such trifle. I pictured to myself with exasperating plainness that this imperious creature, so cold, so aloof—for whom I was to be a mere instrument, and, apart from that, of no more significance to her than the dirt beneath her feet—must, only two or three months before, have been passionate enough when clasped in the arms of the father of this unborn child she now wished me to destroy. Such was the thought which obsessed me. She had approached me with supercilious contempt; but I would make her mine with all the virile masterfulness and impetus and ardour of that unknown man. This is what I want you to grasp. Never before had I tried to take advantage of my position as doctor. If I did so now, it was not from lust, not from an animal longing for sexual possession. I assure you it was not. I was moved by the craving to master her pride, to prove myself a dominant male, and thus to assert the supremacy of my ego over hers.

"I have already told you that arrogant, seemingly cold women have always exercised a peculiar power over me. Superadded to this, on the present occasion, was the fact that for seven years I had not had a white woman in my

arms, had never encountered resistance in my wooing.
Native girls are timorous little creatures who tremble
with respectful ecstasy when a 'white lord,' a 'tuan,' deigns
to take possession of them. They are overflowing with
humility, always ready to give themselves for the asking
—with a servility that robs voluptuousness of its tang.
The Arab girls are different, I believe, and perhaps even
the Chinese and the Malays; but I had been living among
the Javanese. You can understand, then, how thrilled I
was by this woman, so haughty and fierce and reserved;
so brim-full of mystery, and gravid with the fruit of a
recent passion. You can realize what it meant to me that
such a woman should walk boldly into the cage of such
a man as I—a veritable beast, lonely, starved, cut off
from human fellowship. I tell you all this that you may
understand what follows. Those were the thoughts that
coursed through my brain, those were the impulses that
stirred me, when, simulating indifference, I said coolly:

"'One hundred thousand gulden? No, I won't do it
for that.'

"She looked at me, paling a little. No doubt she felt
intuitively that the obstacle was not a matter of money.
All she said, however, was:

"'What fee do you ask, then?'

"'Let's be frank with one another,' I rejoined. 'I am no
trader. You must not look upon me as the poverty-stricken
apothecary in *Romeo and Juliet* who vends poison for
the "worse poison," gold. You will never get what you
want from me if you regard me as a mere man of business.'

"'You won't do it, then?'

"'Not for money.'

"For a moment there was silence. The room was so still that I could hear her breathing.

" 'What else can you want?'

"I answered hotly:

" 'I want, first of all, that you should approach me, not as a trader, but as a man. That when you need help you should come to me, not with a parade of your gold "that's poison to men's souls," but with a prayer to me, the human being, that I should help you, the human being. I am not only a doctor. "Hours of Consultation" are not the only hours I have to dispose of. There are other hours as well—and you may have chanced upon me in one of those other hours.'

"A brief silence followed. Then she pursed up her lips, and said:

" 'So you would do it if I were to implore you?'

" 'I did not say so. You are still trying to bargain, and will only plead if you have my implied promise. Plead first, and then I will answer you.'

"She tossed her head defiantly, like a spirited horse.

" 'I will not plead for your help. I would rather die.'

"I saw red, and answered furiously:

" 'If you will not sue, I will demand. I think there is no need of words. You know already what I want. When you have given it, I will help you.'

"She stared at me for a moment. Then (how can I make you realize the horror of it?) the tension of her features relaxed and she burst out laughing. She laughed with a contempt which at once ground me to powder and intoxicated me to madness. It came like an explosion of incredible violence, this disdainful laughter; and its effect on me was such that I wanted to abase myself before her, longed to kiss her feet. The energy of her scorn blasted me like lightning—and in that instant she turned, and made for the door.

"Involuntarily I pursued her to mumble excuses, to pray forgiveness, so crushed was I in spirit. But she faced me before leaving, to say, to command:

" 'Do not dare to follow me, or try to find out who I am. If you do, you will repent it.'

"In a flash, she was gone."

Further hesitation. Another silence. Then the voice issued from the darkness once more.

"She vanished through the doorway, and I stood rooted to the spot. I was, as it were, hypnotized by her prohibition. I heard her going downstairs; I heard the house-door close; I heard everything. I longed to follow her. Why? I don't know whether it was to call her back, to strike her, to strangle her. Anyhow, I wanted to follow her—and could not. It was as if her fierce answer had paralysed me. I know this will sound absurd; such, however, was the fact. Minutes passed—five, ten, it may be—before I could stir.

"But as soon as I made the first movement, the spell was broken. I rushed down the stairs. There was only one road by which she could have gone, first to the settlement, and thence back to civilization. I hastened to the shed to get my bicycle, only to find that I had forgotten the key. Without waiting to fetch it I dragged the frail bamboo door from its hinges and seized the wheel. Next moment I was pedalling madly down the road in pursuit. I must catch her up; I must overtake her before she could get to her car; I must speak to her.

"The dusty track unrolled itself in front of me, and

the distance I had to ride before I caught sight of her
showed me how long I must have stood entranced after
she left. There she was at last, where the road curved
round the forest just before entering the settlement. She
was walking quickly; behind her strode the China boy.
She must have become aware of my pursuit the instant I
saw her, for she stopped to speak to the boy and then went
on alone, while he stood waiting. Why did she go on
alone? Did she want to speak to me where no one could
listen? I put on a spurt, when suddenly the boy, as I was
about to pass him, leapt in front of me. I swerved to avoid
him, ran up the bank, and fell.

"I was on my feet again in an instant, cursing the boy,
and I raised my fist to deal him a blow, but he evaded it.
Not bothering about him any more, I picked up my bicycle and was about to remount when the rascal sprang
forward and seized the handle-bar, saying in pidgin-
English:

" 'Master stoppee here.'

"You haven't lived in the tropics. You can hardly realize the intolerable impudence of such an action on the
part of a native, and a servant at that. A yellow beast of a
China boy actually presumed to catch hold of my bicycle
and to tell me, a white 'tuan,' to stay where I was! My
natural answer was to give him one between the eyes. He
staggered, but maintained his grip on the cycle. His slit-
like, slanting eyes were full of slavish fear, but for all that
he was stout of heart, and would not let go.

" 'Master stoppee here!' he repeated.

"It was lucky I had not brought my automatic pistol.
Had I had it with me, I should have shot him then and
there.

" 'Let go, you dog!' I shouted.

"He stared at me, panic-stricken, but would not obey. In a fury, and feeling sure that further delay would enable her to escape me, I gave him a knock-out blow on the chin, which crumpled him up in the road.

"Now the cycle was free; but, when I tried to mount, I found that the front wheel had been buckled in the fall and would not turn. After a vain attempt to straighten the wheel, I flung the machine in the dust beside the China boy (who, bleeding from my violence, was coming to his senses) and ran along the road into the settlement.

"Yes, I ran; and here again, you, who have not lived in the tropics, will find it hard to realize all that this implies. For a white man, a European, thus to forget his dignity, and to run before a lot of staring natives, is to make himself a laughing-stock. Well, I was past thinking of my dignity. I ran like a madman in front of the huts, where the inmates gaped to see the settlement doctor, the white lord, running like a rickshaw coolie.

"I was dripping with sweat when I reached the settlement.

" 'Where's the car?' I shouted breathless.

" 'Just gone, Tuan,' came the answer.

"They were staring at me in astonishment. I must have looked like a lunatic, wet and dirty, as I shouted out my question the moment I was within hail. Glancing down the road I saw, no longer the car, but the dust raised by its passing. She had made good her escape. Her device of leaving the boy to hinder me had been successful.

"Yet, after all, her flight availed her nothing. In the tropics the names and the doings of the scattered members of the ruling European caste are known to all. From this outlook, Java is but a big village where gossip is rife. While she had been visiting me, her chauffeur had spent an idle hour in the settlement headquarters. Within a few minutes I knew everything; knew her name, and that she lived in the provincial capital more than a hundred and fifty miles away. She was (as, indeed, I knew already) an Englishwoman. Her husband was a Dutch merchant, fabulously rich. He had been away five months, on a business journey in America, and was expected back in a few days. Then husband and wife were to pay a visit to England.

"Her husband had been five months away. It had been obvious to me that she could not be more than three months pregnant."

"Till now it has been easy enough for me to explain everything to you clearly, for up to this point my motives were plain to myself. As a doctor, a trained observer, I could readily diagnose my own condition. But from now on I was like a man in delirium. I had completely lost self-control. I knew how preposterous were my actions, and yet I went on doing them. Have you ever heard of 'running amuck'?"

"Yes, I think so. It's some sort of drunken frenzy among the Malays, isn't it?"

"More than drunkenness. More than frenzy. It's a condition which makes a man behave like a rabid dog, transforms him into a homicidal maniac. It's a strange and terrible mental disorder. I've seen cases of it and studied them carefully while in the East, without ever being able to clear up its true nature. It's partly an outcome of the climate, of the sultry, damp, oppressive atmosphere, which strains the nerves until at last they snap. Of course a Malay who runs amuck has generally been in trouble of some sort—jealousy, gambling losses, or what not. The man will be sitting quietly, as if there were nothing wrong—just as I was sitting in my room before she came to see me.

"Suddenly he will spring to his feet, seize his kris, dash into the street, and run headlong, no matter where. He stabs any who happen to find themselves in his path, and the shedding of blood infuriates him more and more. He foams at the mouth, shouts as he runs, tears on and on, brandishing his blood-stained dagger. Every one knows that nothing but death will stop the madman; they scurry out of his way, shouting 'Amok, Amok,' to warn others. Thus he runs, killing, killing, killing, until he is shot down like the mad dog that he is.

"It is because I have seen Malays running amuck that I know so well what was my condition during those days, those days still so recent, those days about which I am going to tell you. Like such a Malay, I ran my furious course in pursuit of that Englishwoman, looking neither to the right nor to the left, obsessed with the one thought of seeing her again. I can scarcely remember all I did in the hurried moments before I actually set out on her trail. Within a minute or two of learning her name and where she lived, I had borrowed a bicycle and was racing back to my own quarters. I flung a spare suit or two into a valise, stuffed a bundle of notes into my pocket, and rode off to the nearest railway station. I did not report to the district officer; I made no arrangements about a substitute; I left the house just as it was, paying no heed to the servants who gathered round me asking for instructions. Within an hour from the time when that woman had first called to see me, I had broken with the past and was running amuck into the void.

"In truth I gained nothing by my haste, as I should

have known had I been able to think. It was late afternoon when I got to the railway station, and in the Javanese mountains the trains do not run after dark for fear
of wash-outs. After a sleepless night in the dak-bungalow
and a day's journey by rail, at six in the evening I reached
the town where she lived, feeling sure that, by car, she
would have got there long before me. Within ten minutes I was at her door. 'What could have been more
senseless?' you will say. I know, I know; but one who is
running amuck runs amuck; he does not look where he
is going.

"I sent in my card. The servant (not the China boy—
I suppose he had not turned up yet) came back to say that
his mistress was not well enough to see any one.

"I stumbled into the street. For an hour or more I hung
around the house, in the forlorn hope that perhaps she
would relent and would send out for me. Then I took a
room at a neighbouring hotel and had a couple of bottles
of whiskey sent upstairs. With these and a stiff dose of
veronal I at length managed to drug myself into uncon-
sciousness—a heavy sleep that was the only interlude in
the race from life to death."

Eight bells struck. It was four in the morning. The
sudden noise startled the narrator, and he broke off
abruptly. In a little while, however, collecting himself, he
went on with his story.

"It is hard to describe the hours that followed. I think
I must have had fever. Anyhow I was in a state of irrita-
bility bordering on madness. I was running amuck. It
was on Tuesday evening that I got to the coast town, and,
as I learned next morning, her husband was expected on
Saturday. There were three clear days during which I

might help her out of her trouble. I knew there wasn't a
moment to waste—and she wouldn't see me! My longing
to help, and my longing (still greater, if possible) to excuse myself for my insane demand, intensified the disorder of my nerves. Every second was precious. The whole
thing hung by a hair, and I had behaved so outrageously
that she would not let me come near her. Imagine that
you are running after some one to warn him against an
assassin, and that he takes you for the would-be assassin,
so that he flees from you towards destruction. All that she
could see in me was the frenzied pursuer who had hu-
miliated her with a base proposal and now wanted to re-
new it.

"That was the absurdity of the whole thing. My one
wish was to help her, and she would not see me. I would
have committed any crime to help her, but she did not
know.

"Next morning when I called, the China boy was standing at the door. I suppose that he had got back by the
same train as myself. He must have been on the look-out;
for the instant I appeared he whisked out of sight—
though not before I had seen the bruises on his face. Perhaps he had only hurried in to announce my coming.
That is one of the things that maddens me now, to think
that she may have realized that, after all, I wanted to
help, and may have been ready to receive me. But the
sight of him reminded me of my shame, so that I turned
back from the door without venturing to send in my
name. I went away; went away in torment, when she, perhaps, in no less torment, was awaiting me.

"I did not know how to pass the weary hours in this
unfamiliar town. At length it occurred to me to call on
the Vice-Resident, the man whose leg I had set to rights

up country after he had had a motor smash. He was at home, and was, of course, delighted to see me. Did I tell you that I can speak Dutch as fluently as any Dutchman? I was at school in Holland for a couple of years. That was one reason why I chose the Dutch colonial service when I had to clear out of Leipzig.

"There must have been something queer about my manner, though. My grateful patient, for all his civility, eyed me askance, as if he divined that I was running amuck! I told him I had come to ask for a transfer. I couldn't live in the wilds any longer. I wanted an instant remove to the provincial capital. He looked at me questioningly, and in a noncommittal way—much as a medical man looks at a patient.

" 'A nervous break-down, Doctor?' he inquired. 'I understand that only too well. We can arrange matters for you, but you'll have to wait for a little while; three or four weeks, let us say, while we're finding some one to relieve you at your present post.'

" 'Three or four weeks!' I exclaimed. 'I can't wait a single day!'

"Again that questioning look.

" 'I'm afraid you'll have to put up with it, Doctor. We mustn't leave your station unattended. Still, I promise you I'll set matters in train this very day.'

"I stood there biting my lips and realizing for the first time how completely I had sold myself into slavery. It was in my mind to defy him and his regulations; but he was tactful, he was indebted to me, and he did not want an open breach. Forestalling my determination to reply angrily, he went on:

" 'You've been living like a hermit, you know, and that's enough to put any one's nerves on edge. We've all been wondering why you never asked for leave, why you never came to see us down here. Some cheerful company, now and then, would have done you all the good in the world. This evening, by the way, there's a reception at Government House. Won't you join us? The whole colony will be there, including a good many people who have often asked about you, and have wanted very much to make your acquaintance.'

"At this I pricked up my ears. 'Asked about me?' 'Wanted to make my acquaintance?' Was she one of them? The thought was like wine to me. I remembered my manners, thanked him for his invitation, and promised to come early.

"I did go early, too early! Spurred on by impatience, I was the first to appear in the great drawing-room at the Residency. There I had to sit cooling my heels and listening to the soft tread of the bare-footed native servants who went to and fro about their business and (so it seemed to my morbid imagination) were sniggering at me behind my back. For a quarter of an hour I was the only guest amid a silence which, when the servants had finished their preparations, became so profound that I could hear the ticking of my watch in my pocket.

"Then the other guests began to arrive, some government officials with their wives, and the Vice-Resident put in an appearance. He welcomed me most graciously, and entered into a long conversation, in which (I think) I was able to keep my end up all right—until, of a sudden, my nervousness returned, and I began to falter.

"She had entered the room, and it was a good thing that at this moment the Vice-Resident wound up his talk with me and began a conversation with some one else, for otherwise I believe I should simply have turned my back

on the man. She was dressed in yellow silk, which set off
her ivory shoulders admirably, and was talking brightly
amid a group. Yet I, who knew her secret trouble, could
read (or fancied I could read) care beneath her smile. I
moved nearer, but she did not or would not see me. That
smile of hers maddened me once more, for I knew it to
be feigned. 'Today is Wednesday,' I thought. 'On Saturday her husband will be back. How can she smile so un-
concernedly? How can she toy with her fan, instead of
breaking it with a convulsive clutch?'

"I, a stranger, was trembling in face of what awaited
her. I, a stranger, had for two days been suffering with
her suffering. What could her smile be but a mask to hide
the storm that raged within?

"From the next room came the sound of music. Dancing was to begin. A middle-aged officer claimed her as his
partner. Excusing herself to those with whom she had
been conversing, she took his arm and walked with him
towards the ballroom. This brought her close to me, and
she could not fail to see me. For a moment she was startled,
and then (before I could make up my mind whether or
not to claim acquaintance) she nodded in a friendly way,
said 'Good evening, Doctor,' and passed on.

"No one could have guessed what lay hidden behind
that casual glance. Indeed, I myself was puzzled. Why had
she openly recognized me? Was she making an advance,
an offer of reconciliation? Was she still on the defensive?
Had she merely been taken by surprise? How could I
tell? All I knew was that I had been stirred to the depths.

"I watched her as she waltzed, a smile of enjoyment
playing about her lips, and I knew that all the while she
must be thinking, not of the dance, but of the one thing
of which I was thinking, of the dread secret which she and

I alone shared. The thought intensified (if possible) my anxiety, my longing, and my bewilderment. I don't know if any one else was observing me, but I am sure that my eager scrutiny of her must have been in manifest contrast to her ostensible unconcern. I simply could not look at any one but her, for I was watching all the time to see whether she would not, were it but for a moment, let the mask fall. The fixity of my stare must have been disagreeable to her. As she came back on her partner's arm, she flashed a look at me, dictatorial, angry, as if bidding me to exercise a little more self-control.

"But I, as I have explained to you, was running amuck. I knew well enough what her glance meant! 'Don't attract attention to me like this. Keep yourself in hand.' She was asking me to show some discretion in this place of public assembly. I felt assured, now, that if I went quietly home she would receive me should I call on the morrow; that all she wanted of me was that I should behave decorously; that she was (with good reason) afraid of my making a scene. Yes, I understood what she wanted; but I was running amuck, and I had to speak to her there and then. I moved over to the group amid which she was talking. They were all strangers to me; yet I rudely shouldered my way in among them. There I stood my ground listening to her, though I trembled like a whipped cur whenever her eyes rested coldly on mine. I was obviously unwelcome. No one said a word to me, and it must have been plain that she resented my intrusion.

"I cannot tell how long I should have gone on standing there. To all eternity, perhaps. I was spellbound. To her, however, the strain became unbearable. Suddenly she broke off, and, with a charming and convincing assumption of indifference, said: 'Well, I'm rather tired, so

I shall turn in early. I'll ask you to excuse me. Good night!'

"She gave a friendly nod which included me with the others, and turned away. I watched her smooth, white, well-shaped back above her yellow silk gown, and at first (so dazed was I) I scarcely realized that I was to see her no more that evening, that I was to have no word with her on that last evening to which I had looked forward as the evening of salvation. I stood stock-still until I grasped this. Then . . . then . . .

"I must put the whole picture before you, if I am to make you understand what an idiot I made of myself. The big drawing-room at the Residency was now almost empty, though blazing with light. Most of the guests were dancing in the ballroom, while the older men who had lost taste for pairing off in this way had settled down to cards elsewhere. There were but a few scattered groups talking here and there. Across this huge hall she walked, with that dignity and grace which enthralled me, nodding farewell to one and to another as she passed. By the time I had fully taken in the situation, she was at the other end of the room and about to leave it. At that instant, becoming aware that she would escape me, I started to run after her, yes, to run, my pumps clattering as I sped across the polished floor. Of course every one stared at me, and I was overwhelmed with shame—yet I could not stop. I caught her up as she reached the door, and she turned on me, her eyes blazing, her nostrils quivering with scorn.

"But she had the self-command which in me was so lamentably lacking, and in an instant she had mastered her anger and burst out laughing. With ready wit, speaking loudly so that all could hear, she said:

" 'Ah, Doctor, so you've just remembered that prescription for my little boy, after all! You men of science are apt to be forgetful now and again, aren't you?'

"Two men standing near by grinned good-humouredly. I understood, admired the skill with which she was glossing over my clownishness, and had the sense to take her hint. Pulling out my pocketbook, in which there were some prescription blanks, I tore one off and handed it to her with a muttered apology. Taking the paper from me with a smile and a 'Good night!' she departed.

"She had saved the situation; but I felt that, as far as my position with her was concerned, the case was hopeless, that she loathed me for my insensate folly, hated me more than death; that again and again and again (however often I might come) she would drive me from her door like a dog.

"I stumbled across the room, people staring at me. No doubt there was something strange about my appearance. Making my way to the buffet, I drank four glasses of brandy in brief succession. My nerves were worn to rags, and nothing but this overdose of stimulant would have kept me going. I slipped away by a side door, furtively, as if I had been a burglar. Not for a kingdom would I have crossed the great hall again, have exposed myself to mocking eyes. What did I do next? I can hardly remember. Wandering from one saloon to another, I tried to drink myself into oblivion; but nothing could dull my senses. Still I heard the laugh which had first driven me crazy, and the feigned laughter with which she had covered up my boorishness that evening. Walking on the quays, I looked down into the water, and regretted bitterly that I had not brought my pistol with me, so that I could blow out my brains and drop into the quiet pool. My mind became fixed on this automatic, and I resolved to make an end of myself. I wearily went back to the hotel.

"If I refrained from shooting myself in the small hours, it was not, believe me, from cowardice. Nothing I should have liked better than to press the trigger, in the conviction that thus I could put an end to the torment of my thoughts. After all, I was obsessed by the idea of duty, that accursed notion of duty. It maddened me to think that she might still have need of me, to know that she really did need me. Here was Thursday morning. In two days her husband would be back. I was sure this proud woman would never live to face the shame that must ensue upon discovery. I tramped up and down my room for hours, turning these thoughts over in my mind, cursing the impatience, the blunders, that had made it impossible for me to help her. How was I to approach her now? How was I to convince her that all I asked was to be allowed to serve her? She would not see me, she would not see me. In fancy I heard her fierce laughter, and watched her nostrils twitching with contempt. Up and down, up and down the ten feet of my narrow room, till the tropic day had dawned, and, speedily, the morning sun was glaring into the veranda. As you know, in the tropics every one is up and about by six.

"Flinging myself into a chair, I seized some letter-paper and began to write to her, anything, everything, a cringing letter, in which I implored her forgiveness, proclaimed myself a madman and a villain, besought her to trust me, to put herself in my hands after all. I swore that I would disappear thereafter, from the town, the colony, the world, if she wanted me to. Let her only forgive me and trust me, allow me to help her in this supreme moment.

"I covered twenty pages. It must have been a fantastic letter, like one penned in a lunatic asylum, or by a man in the delirium of fever. When I had finished, I was dripping with sweat, and the room whirled round me as I rose to my feet. Gulping down a glass of water, I tried to read through what I had written, but the words swam before my eyes. I reached for an envelope, and then it occurred to me to add something that might move her. Snatching up the pen once more, I scrawled across the back of the last page: 'Shall await a word of forgiveness here at the hotel. If I don't hear from you before nightfall, I shall shoot myself.'

"Closing the letter, I shouted for one of the boys and told him to have the chit delivered instantly. There was nothing more for me to do but to await an answer."

As if to mark this interval, it was some minutes before he spoke again. When he did so, the words came with a renewed impetus.

"Christianity has lost its meaning for me. The old myths of heaven and hell no longer influence me. But if there were a hell, I should dread it little, for there could be no hell worse than those hours I spent in the hotel. A little room, baking in the noonday heat. You know these hotel rooms in the tropics—only a bed and a table and a chair. Nothing on the table but a watch and an automatic. Sitting on the chair in front of the table a man staring at the watch and the pistol—a man who ate nothing, drank nothing, did not even smoke, but sat without stirring as he looked at the dial of his watch and saw the second hand making its unending circuit. That was how I spent the day, waiting, waiting, waiting. And yet, for all that I was motionless, I was still like the Malay running amuck, or like a rabid dog, pursuing my frenzied course to destruction.

"Well, I won't make any further attempt to describe those hours. Enough to say that I don't understand how any one can live through such a time and keep reasonably sane.

"At twenty-two minutes past three (my eyes were still glued to the watch) there came a knock at the door. A native youngster with a folded scrap of paper—no envelope. I snatched it from him, and he was gone before I had time to open the note. Then, to begin with, I could not read the brief message. Here was her reply at last, and the words ran together before my eyes! They conveyed no meaning to me. I had to dip my head in cold water and calm my agitation before my senses cleared and I could grasp the meaning of the pencilled English.

" 'Too late! Still, you'd better stay at the hotel. Perhaps I shall have to send for you in the end.'

"There was no signature on the crumpled page, a blank half-sheet torn from a prospectus or something of the kind. The writing was unsteady, perhaps from agitation, perhaps because it had been written in a moving carriage. How could I tell? All I knew was that anxiety, haste, horror, seemed to cling to it; that it gripped me profoundly; and yet that I was glad, for at least she had written to me. I was to keep alive, for she might need me, she might let me help her after all. I lost myself in the maddest conjectures and hopes. I read the curt words again and again; I kissed them repeatedly; I grew calmer, and passed into a state betwixt sleep and waking when time no longer had any meaning—coma-vigil is what we doctors call it.

"This must have lasted for hours. Dusk was at hand when I came to myself with a start, so it was certainly near

six o'clock. Had there been another knock? I listened intently. Then it was unmistakable—a knocking, gentle yet
insistent. Unsteadily (for I felt giddy and faint) I sprang
to the door. There in the passage stood the China boy. It
was still light enough to show me, not only the traces of
my rough handling, not only black eyes and a bruised
chin, but that his yellow face was ashen pale.

" 'Master come quickly.' That was all.

"I ran downstairs, the boy at my heels. A gharry was
waiting, and we jumped in.

" 'What has happened?' I asked, as the man drove off,
without further orders.

"The boy looked at me, his lips twitched, but he said
never a word. I repeated my questions; still he was silent.
I felt angry enough to strike him once more; yet I was
touched by his devotion to his mistress, and so I kept myself in hand. If he wouldn't speak, he wouldn't; that was
all.

"The gharryman was flogging his ponies, driving so
furiously that people had to jump out of the way to avoid
being run over. The streets were thronged, for we had
left the European settlement, and were on our way
through the Javanese and Malay town into the Chinese
quarter. Here the gharry drew up in a narrow alley, in
front of a tumbledown house. It was a sordid place, a
little shop in front, lighted by a tallow candle; the
attached dwelling was an unsavoury hotel—one of those
opium-dens, brothels, thieves' kitchens, or receivers'
stores, such as are run by the worser sort of Chinese in all
the big cities of the East.

"The boy knocked at the door. It opened for an inch
or two, and a tedious parley ensued. Impatiently I, too,
jumped out of the gharry, put my shoulder to the door,

forced it open—an elderly Chinese woman fled before me with a shriek. I dashed along a passage, the boy after me, to another door. Opening this, I found myself in a dim interior, reeking of brandy and of blood. Some one was groaning. I could make out nothing in the gloom, but I groped my way towards the sound."

Another pause. When he spoke again, it was with sobs almost as much as with words.

"I groped my way towards the sound—and there she was, lying on a strip of dirty matting, twisted with pain, sighing and groaning. I could not see her face, so dark was the room. Stretching out my hand, I found hers, which was burning hot. She was in a high fever. I shuddered as I realized what had happened. She had come to this foul den in quest of the service I had refused, had sought out a Chinese midwife, hoping in this way to find the secrecy she no longer trusted me to observe. Rather than place herself in my care, she had come to the old witch I had seen in the passage, had had herself mauled by a bungler —because I had behaved like a madman, had so grievously affronted her that she thought it better to take any risks rather than to let me give the aid which, to begin with, I had only been willing to grant on monstrous terms.

"I shouted for light, and that detestable beldame brought a stinking and smoky kerosene lamp. I should have liked to strangle her—but what good would that have done? She put the lamp down on the table; and now, in its yellow glare, I could see the poor, martyred body.

"Then, of a sudden, the fumes were lifted from my brain. No longer half crazed, I forgot my anger, and even for the time forgot the evil mood that had brought us to this pass. Once more I was the doctor, the man of skill and knowledge, to whom there had come an urgent call to use them for the best advantage of a suffering fellow-mortal. I forgot my wretched self; and, with reawakened intelligence, I was ready to do battle with the forces of destruction.

"I passed my hands over the nude body which so recently I had lusted for. Now it had become the body of my patient, and was nothing more. I saw in it only the seat of a life at grips with death, only the form of one writhing in torment. Her blood on my hands was not horrible to me, now that I was again the expert upon whose coolness everything turned. I saw, as an expert, the greatness of her danger. . . .

"I saw, indeed, that all was lost, short of a miracle. She had been so mishandled that her life-blood was rapidly draining away. And what was there, in this filthy hovel, which I could make use of in the hope of stanching the flow? Everything I looked at, everything I touched, was besoiled. Not even a clean basin and clean water!

" 'We must have you removed to hospital instantly,' I said. Thereupon, torture of mind superadded to torture of body, she writhed protestingly.

" 'No,' she whispered, 'no, no. I would rather die. No one must know. No one must know. Take me home, home!'

"I understood. Her reputation was more to her than her life. I understood, and I obeyed. The boy fetched a litter. We lifted her on to it, and then carried her, half dead, home through the night. Ignoring the terrified questions and exclamations of the servants, we took her to her room. Then began the struggle; the prolonged and futile struggle with death."

He clutched my arm, so that it was hard not to shout from surprise and pain. His face was so close that I could see the white gleam of teeth and the pale sheen of spectacle-glasses in the starlight. He spoke with such intensity, with such fierce wrath, that his voice assailed me like something betwixt a hiss and a shriek.

"You, a stranger I have never glimpsed in the daylight, you who are (I suppose) touring the world at your ease, do you know what it is to see some one die? Have you ever sat by any one in the death agony, seen the body twisting in the last wrestle and the blue fingernails clawing at vacancy; heard the rattle in the throat; watched the inexpressible horror in the eyes of the dying? Have you ever had that terrible experience—you, an idler, a globe-trotter, who can talk so glibly about one's duty to help?

"I have seen it often enough as a doctor, have studied death as a clinical happening. Once only have I experienced it in the full sense of the term. Once only have I lived with another and died with another. Once only, during that ghastly vigil a few nights ago when I sat cudgelling my brains for some way of stopping the flow of blood, some means of cooling the fever which was consuming her before my eyes, some method of staving off imminent death.

"Do you understand what it is to be a doctor, thoroughly trained in the science and practice of medicine, and (as you sagely remark) one whose first duty is to help —and to sit powerless by the bedside of the dying; knowing, for all one's knowledge, only one thing—that one can give no help? To feel the pulse as it flickers and fades? My hands were tied! I could not take her to the hospital, where something might have been done to give her a chance. I could not summon aid. I could only sit and watch her die, mumbling meaningless invocations like an old applewoman at church, and next minute clenching my fists in impotent wrath against a non-existent deity.

"Can you understand? Can you understand? What I cannot understand is how one survives such hours, why one does not die with the dying, how one can get up next morning and clean one's teeth and put on one's necktie; how one can go on living in the ordinary way after feeling what I had felt, for the first time, that one I would give anything and everything to save was slipping away, somewhither, beyond recall.

"There was an additional torment. As I sat beside the bed (I had given her an injection of morphine to ease the pain, and she lay quiet now, with cheeks ashen pale), I felt the unceasing tension of a fixed gaze boring into my back. The China boy was sitting cross-legged on the floor, murmuring prayers in his own tongue. Whenever I glanced at him, he raised his eyes imploringly to mine, like a hound dumbly beseeching aid. He lifted his hands as if in supplication to a god—lifted them to me, the impotent weakling who knew that all was vain, that I was of no more use in that room than an insect running across the floor.

"It added to my torture, this petitioning of his, this fanatical conviction that my skill would enable me to save the woman whose life was ebbing as he looked on and prayed. I could have screamed at him and have trampled him under foot, so much did his eager expectancy hurt me; and yet I felt that he and I were bound together by our fondness for the dying woman and by the dread secret we shared.

"Like an animal at watch, he sat huddled up behind me; but the instant I wanted anything he was alert, eager to fetch it, hoping I had thought of something that might help even now. He would have given his own blood to save her life. I am sure of it. So would I. But what was the use of thinking of transfusion (even if I had had the instruments) when there were no means of arresting the flow of blood? It would only have prolonged her agony. But this China boy would have died for her, as would I. Such was the power she had. And I had not even the power to save her from bleeding to death!

"Towards daybreak she regained consciousness, awoke from the drugged sleep. She opened her eyes, which were no longer proud and cold. The heat of fever glowed in them as she looked round the room. Catching sight of me, she was puzzled for a moment, and needed an effort to recall who this stranger was. Then she remembered. She regarded me at first with enmity, waving her arms feebly as if to repel me, and showing by her movements that she would have fled from me had she but had the strength. Then, collecting her thoughts, she looked at me more calmly. Her breathing was laboured; she tried to speak; she wanted to sit up, but was too weak. Begging her to desist, I leaned closer to her, so that I should be able to hear her lightest whisper. She regarded me piteously, her lips moved, and faint indeed was the whisper that came from them:

" 'No one will find out? No one?'

" 'No one,' I responded, with heartfelt conviction. 'No one shall ever know.'

"Her eyes were still uneasy. With a great effort she managed to breathe the words:

" 'Swear that no one shall know. Swear it.'

"I raised my hand solemnly and murmured: 'I pledge you my word.'

"She looked at me, weak though she was, cordially, gratefully. Yes, despite all the harm I had done, she was grateful to me at the last, she smiled her thanks. A little later she tried to speak again, but was not equal to the exertion. Then she lay peacefully, with her eyes closed. Before daylight shone clearly into the room, all was over."

A long silence. He had overcome the frenzy which had prompted him to seize me by the arm, and had sunk back exhausted. The stars were paling when three bells struck. A fresh though gentle breeze was blowing as herald of the dawn that comes so quickly in the tropics. Soon I could see him plainly. He had taken off his cap, so that his face was exposed. It was pinched with misery. He scanned me through his spectacles with some interest, to see what sort of man was this stranger to whom he had been pouring out his heart. Then he went on with his story, speaking with a scornful intonation.

"For her, all was over; but not for me. I was alone with the corpse, in a strange house; in a town where (as in all such places) gossip runs like wildfire, and I had pledged my word that her secret should be kept! Consider the situation. Here was a woman moving in the best society of the colony, and, to all seeming, in perfect health. She had danced the evening before last at Government House. Now she was dead, and the only doctor who knew anything about the matter, the man who had sat by her while she died, was a chance visitor to the town, summoned to her bedside by one of the servants. This doctor and this servant had brought her home in a litter under cover of darkness and had kept every one else out of the way. Not until morning did they call the other servants, to tell them their mistress was dead. The news would be all over the

town within an hour or two, and how was I, the doctor
from an up-country station, to account for the sudden
death, for what I had done and for what I had failed to
do? Why hadn't I sent for one of my colleagues to share
the responsibility? Why? . . . Why? . . . Why?

"I knew what lay before me. My only helper was the
China boy; but he, at any rate, was a devoted assistant,
who realized that there was still a fight to be fought.

"I had said to him: 'You understand, don't you? Your
mistress's last wish was that no one shall know what has
happened.'

" 'Savee plenty, Master,' he answered simply; and I
knew that I could trust him.

"He washed the blood stains from the floor, set all to
rights as quickly as possible, and his fortitude sustained
mine.

"Never before have I had so much concentrated energy,
nor shall I ever have it again. When one has lost everything but a last remnant, one fights for that last remnant
with desperate courage, with fierce resolution. The remnant for which I was fighting was her legacy to me, her
secret. I was calm and self-assured in my reception of
every one who came, telling them the tale I had decided
upon to account for the death. After all, people are used
to sudden, grave, and fatal illness in the tropics; and the
laity cannot openly question a doctor's authoritative state-
ments. I explained that the China boy, whom she had
sent to fetch the doctor when she was taken ill, had
chanced to meet me. But while talking thus to all and
sundry with apparent composure, I was awaiting the one
man who really mattered, the senior surgeon, who would
have to inspect the body before burial could take place.
It was Thursday morning, and on Saturday the husband

was coming back. Speedy burial is the rule in this part of the world; but the senior surgeon, not I, would have to sign the necessary certificates.

"At nine he was announced. I had sent for him, of course. He was my superior in rank, and he bore me a grudge because of the local reputation I had acquired in the little matter of the Vice-Resident's broken leg. This was the doctor of whom she had spoken so contemptuously, as good only for bridge. According to official routine my wish for a transfer would pass through his hands. No doubt the Vice-Resident had already mentioned it to him.

"The instant we met that morning, I guessed his enmity, but this only steeled me to my task.

"As soon as I came into the ante-room where he was waiting, he began the attack.

" 'When did Madame Blank die?'

" 'At six this morning.'

" 'When did she send for you?'

" 'At nightfall yesterday.'

" 'Did you know that I was her regular professional attendant?'

" 'Yes.'

" 'Why didn't you send for me, then?'

" 'There wasn't time—and, besides, Madame Blank had put herself in my hands exclusively. In fact, she expressly forbade me to call in any other doctor.'

"He stared at me. His face flushed. Suppressing an angry retort, he said with assumed indifference:

" 'Well, even though you could get on without me so long as she was alive, you have fulfilled your official duty in sending for me now, and I must fulfil mine by verifying the death and ascertaining the cause.'

"I made no answer, and let him lead the way to the death-chamber. As soon as we were there, and before he could touch the body, I said:

" 'It is not a question of ascertaining the cause of death, but of inventing a cause. Madame Blank sent for me to save her, if I could, from the consequences of an abortion, clumsily performed by a Chinese midwife. To save her life was impossible, but I pledged my word to save her reputation. I want you to help me.'

"He looked his surprise.

" 'You actually want me, the senior surgeon of this province, to join you in concealing a crime?'

" 'Yes, that is what I want you to do.'

" 'In fact,' he said with a sneer, 'I am to help in the hushing-up of a crime you have committed.'

" 'I have given you to understand that, as far as Madame Blank is concerned, all I have done is to try to save her from the consequences of her own indiscretion and some one else's crime (if you want to insist on the word). Had I been the culprit, I should not be alive at this hour. She has herself paid the extreme penalty, and the miserable bungler who procured the abortion really does not matter one way or the other. You cannot punish the criminal without tarnishing the dead woman's reputation, and that I will not suffer.'

" 'You will not suffer it? You talk to me as if you were my official chief, instead of my being yours. You dare to order me about. I had already surmised there must be something queer when you were summoned from your nook in the backwoods. A fine beginning you've made of it with your attempt to interlope here. Well, all that remains for me is to make my own investigation, and I can assure you that I shall report exactly what I find. I'm not going to put my name to a false certificate; you needn't think so!'

"I was imperturbable.

" 'You'll have to, this once. If you don't, you'll never leave the room alive.'

"I put my hand in my pocket. The pistol was not there (I had left it in my room at the hotel), but the bluff worked. He drew back in alarm; whereupon I made a step forward and said, with a calculated mingling of threat and conciliation:

" 'Look here! I shall be sorry to go to extremes, but you'd better understand that I don't value either my life or yours at a single stiver. I'm so far through that there's only one thing in the world left for me to care about, and that's the keeping of my promise to this dead woman that the manner of her death shall remain secret. I give you my word that if you sign a certificate to the effect that she died of—what shall we say?—a sudden access of malignant tropical fever with hyperpyrexia, leading to heart failure —that will sound plausible enough—if you do this, I will leave the Indies within a week. I will, if you like, put a bullet through my head as soon as she is buried and I can be sure that no one (you understand, no one) can make any further examination. That should satisfy you. In fact, it must satisfy you.'

"My voice, my whole aspect, must have been menacing, for he was cowed. Whenever I advanced a little, he retreated, showing that uncontrollable fear with which people flee from a man brandishing a blood-stained kris, a man who is running amuck. He wilted visibly, and changed his tone. He was no longer the adamantine official, standing invincibly upon punctilio.

"Still, with a last vestige of resistance, he murmured:

" 'Never in my life have I signed a false certificate. Perhaps there would be no question raised if I were to word the document as you suggest. It is perfectly clear to me, however, that I ought not to do anything of the kind.'

" 'Of course you "ought not," judging by conventional standards,' I rejoined, wishing to help him to save his face. 'But this is a special case. When you know that the disclosure of the truth can only bring grievous suffering to a living man and blast the reputation of a dead woman, why hesitate?'

"He nodded. We sat down together at the table. Amicable enough now to all seeming, we concocted the certificate which was the basis of the account of the matter published in next day's newspaper. Then he stood up and looked at me searchingly:

" 'You'll sail for Europe by the next boat, won't you?'

" 'Of course! I've pledged you my word.'

"He continued to stare at me. I saw that he wanted to be strict and businesslike, and that the task was hard. It was as much in the endeavour to hide his embarrassment as from any wish to convey information that he said:

" 'Blank was going home with his wife immediately after his arrival from Yokohama. I expect the poor fellow will want to take his wife's body back to her people in England. He's a wealthy man, you know, and the rich can indulge these fancies. I shall order the coffin instantly, and have it lined with sheet lead so that it can be sealed. That will get over immediate difficulties, and he will know that in this sweltering heat there was no possibility of awaiting his appearance on the scene. Even if he thinks we've been precipitate, he won't venture to say so. We're officials, and he's only a merchant after all, though he could buy us both up and never miss the money. Besides, we're acting as we do to save him needless pain.'

"My enemy of a few minutes back was now my acknowledged confederate. Well, he knew he was soon going to be rid of me for ever; and he had to justify himself to himself. But what he did next was utterly unexpected. He shook me warmly by the hand!

" 'I hope you'll soon be all right again,' he said.

"What on earth did he mean? Was I ill? Was I mad? I opened the door for him ceremoniously, and bade him farewell. Therewith my energies ran down. The room swam round me, and I collapsed beside her bed, as the frenzied Malay collapses when he has run his murderous course and is at last shot down.

"I don't know how long I lay on the floor. At length there was a rustling noise, a movement in the room. I looked up. There stood the China boy, regarding me uneasily.

" 'Some one have come. Wanchee see Missee,' he said.

" 'You mustn't let any one in.'

" 'But, Master . . .'

"He hesitated, looked at me timidly, and tried in vain to speak. The poor wretch was obviously suffering.

" 'Who is it?'

"He trembled like a dog in fear of a blow. He did not utter any name. A sense of delicacy rare in a native servant restrained him. He said simply:

" 'B'long that man!'

"He did not need to be explicit. I knew instantly whom he meant. At the word I was all eagerness to see this unknown, whose very existence I had forgotten. For, strange as it may seem to you, after the first disclosure she had made to me and her rejection of my infamous proposal,

I had completely put him out of my mind. Amid the hurry
and anxiety and stress of what had happened since, it had
actually slipped my memory that there was another man
concerned in the affair, the man this woman had loved,
the man to whom she had passionately given what she had
refused to give me. The day before, I should have hated
him, should have longed to tear him to pieces. Now I was
eager to see him because I loved him—yes, loved the man
whom she had loved.

"With a bound I was in the ante-room. A young, very
young, fair-haired officer was standing there, awkward and
shy. He was pale and slender, looking little more than a
boy, and yet touchingly anxious to appear manlike, calm,
and composed. His hand was trembling as he raised it in
salute. I could have put my arms round him and hugged
him, so perfectly did he fulfil my ideal of the man I should
have wished to be this woman's lover—not a self-confident
seducer, but a tender stripling to whom she had thought
fit to give herself.

"He stood before me, abashed. My sudden apparition,
my eager scrutiny, increased his embarrassment. His face
puckered slightly, and it was plain that he was on the
verge of tears.

" 'I don't want to push in,' he said at length, 'but I
should like so much to see Madame Blank once more.'

"Scarcely aware of what I was doing, I put an arm
round the young fellow's shoulders and guided him
towards the door. He looked at me with astonishment,
but with gratitude as well. At this instant we had an in-
dubitable sense of fellowship. We went together to the
bedside. She lay there; all but the head, shoulders, and
arms hidden by the white linen. Feeling that my close-
ness must be distasteful to him, I withdrew to a distance.

Suddenly he collapsed, as I had done; sank to his knees, and, no longer ashamed to show his emotion, burst into tears.

"What could I say? Nothing! What could I do? I raised him to his feet and led him to the sofa. There we sat side by side; and, to soothe him, I gently stroked his soft, blond hair. He took my hand in his and pressed it affectionately. Then he said:

" 'Tell me the whole truth, Doctor. She didn't kill herself, did she?'

" 'No,' I answered.

" 'Then is any one else to blame for her death?'

" 'No,' I said once more, although from within was welling up the answer: 'I, I, I—and you. The two of us. We are to blame. We two—and her unhappy pride.'

"But I kept the words unuttered, and was content to say yet again:

" 'No! No one was to blame. It was her doom.'

" 'I can't realize it,' he groaned. 'It seems incredible. The night before last she was at the ball; she nodded to me and smiled. How could it happen? How did she come to die so unexpectedly, so swiftly?'

"I told him a string of falsehoods. Even from her lover I must keep the secret. We spent that day and the next and the next together in brotherly converse, both aware (though we did not give the knowledge voice) that our lives were intertwined by our relationship to the dead woman. Again and again I found it hard to keep my own counsel, but I did so. He never learned that she had been with child by him; that she had come to me to have the fruit of their love destroyed; and that, after my refusal, she had taken the step which had ended her own life as well. Yet we talked of nothing but her during those days

when I was hidden in his quarters. I had forgotten to
tell you that! They were searching for me. Her husband
had arrived after the coffin had been closed. He was suspicious—all sorts of rumours were afoot—and he wanted
my account of the matter at first hand. But I simply
couldn't endure the thought of meeting him, the man
through whom I knew she had suffered; so I hid myself,
and during four days I never left the house. Her lover
took a passage for me under a false name, and late at
night I went on board the boat bound for Singapore. I
left everything, all my possessions, the work I had done
in the last seven years. My house stood open to any one
who chose to enter it. No doubt the authorities have already erased my name from the list of their officials as
'absent without leave.' But I could not go on living in
that house, that town, that world, where everything reminded me of her. If I fled like a thief in the night it was
to escape her, to forget her.

"Vain was the attempt! When I came on board at midnight, my friend with me to see me off, a great, oblong,
brass-bound chest was being hoisted on board by the
crane. It was her coffin, her coffin! It had followed me,
just as I had followed her down from the hills to the
coast. I could make no sign, I had to look on unheeding,
for her husband was there, too. He was on his way to
England. Perhaps he means to have the coffin opened
when he gets there; to have a post-mortem made; to find
out . . . Anyhow, he has taken her back to him, has
snatched her away from us; she belongs to him now, not
to us. At Singapore, where I transhipped to this German
mail-boat, the coffin was transhipped as well; and he is
here, too, the husband. But I am still watching over her,
and shall watch over her to the end. He shall never learn

her secret. I shall defend her to the last against the man to escape whom she went to her death. He shall learn nothing, nothing. Her secret belongs to me, and to no one else in the world.

"Do you understand? Do you understand why I keep out of the other passengers' way, why I cannot bear to hear them laugh and chatter, to watch their foolish flirtations—when I know that deep down in the hold, among the tea-chests and the cases of brazil nuts, her body lies? I can't get near it, for the hatches are closed; but I feel its nearness by day and by night, when the passengers are tramping up and down the promenade deck or dancing merrily in the saloon. It is stupid of me, I know. The sea ebbs and flows above millions of corpses, and the dead are rotting beneath every spot where one sets foot on land. All the same, I cannot bear it. I cannot bear it when they dance and laugh in this ship which is taking her body home. I know what she expects of me. There is still something left for me to do. Her secret is not yet safe; and, until it is safe, my pledge to her will be unfulfilled."

From midships there came splashing and scraping noises. The sailors were swabbing the decks. He started at the sound, and jumped to his feet.

"I must be going," he murmured.

He was a distressing sight, with his care-worn expression, and his eyes reddened by weeping and by drink. He had suddenly become distant in his manner. Obviously he was regretting his loquacity, was ashamed of himself for having opened his heart to me as he had done. Wishing to be friendly, however, I said:

"Won't you let me pay you a visit in your cabin this afternoon?"

A smile—mocking, harsh, cynical—twisted his lips; and when he answered, after a momentary hesitation, it was with appropriate emphasis.

"Ah, yes, 'it's one's duty to help.' That's your favourite maxim, isn't it? Your use of it a few hours ago, when you caught me in a weak moment, has loosened my tongue finely! Thank you for your good intentions, but I'd rather be left to myself. Don't imagine, either, that I feel any better for having turned myself inside out before you and for having shown you my very entrails. My life has been torn to shreds, and no one can patch it together again. I have gained nothing by working in the Dutch colonial service for seven years. My pension has gone phut, and I am returning to Germany a pauper—like a dog that slinks behind a coffin. A man cannot run amuck without paying for it. In the end, he is shot down; and I hope that for me the end will come soon. I'm obliged to you for proposing to call, but I've the best of companions to prevent my feeling lonely in my cabin—plenty of bottles of excellent whiskey. They're a great consolation. Then there's another old friend, and my only regret is that I didn't make use of it soon instead of late. My automatic, I mean, which will in the end be better for my soul than any amount of open confession. So I won't trouble you to call, if you don't mind. Among the 'rights of man' there is a right which no one can take away, the right to croak when and where and how one pleases, without a 'helping hand.' "

He looked at me scornfully and with a challenging air, but I knew that at bottom his feeling was one of shame, infinite shame. Saying no word of farewell, he turned on his heel, and slouched off in the direction of the cabins. I never saw him again, though I visited the fore-deck sev-

eral times after midnight. So completely did he vanish
that I might have thought myself the victim of hallucina-
tion had I not noticed among the other passengers a man
wearing a crape armlet, a Dutchman, I was told, whose
wife had recently died of tropical fever. He walked apart,
holding converse with no one, and was melancholy of
mien. Watching him, I was distressed by the feeling that
I was aware of his secret trouble. When my path crossed
his, I turned my face away, lest he should divine from
my expression that I knew more about his fate than he did
himself.

In Naples harbour occurred the accident which was
explicable to me in the light of the stranger's tale. Most
of the passengers were, as I have said, ashore at the time.
I had been to the opera, and had then supped in one of
the brightly lit cafés in the Via Roma. As I was being
rowed back to the steamer, I noticed that there was a
commotion going on round the gangway, boats moving
to and fro, and men in them holding torches and acety-
lene lamps as they scanned the water. On deck there were
several carabinieri, talking in low tones. I asked one of
the deck-hands what was the matter. He answered eva-
sively, so that it was obvious he had been told to be discreet. Next morning, too, when we were steaming towards
Genoa, I found it impossible to glean any information.
But at Genoa, in an Italian newspaper, I read a high-
flown account of what had happened that night at Naples.
    Under cover of darkness, it appeared, to avoid disquiet-
ing the passengers, a coffin from the Dutch Indies was being lowered into a boat. It contained the body of a lady;
and her husband (who was taking it home for burial) was
already waiting in the boat. Something heavy had, when

the coffin was half way down the ship's side, dropped on it from the upper deck, carrying it away, so that it fell with a crash into the boat, which instantly capsized. The coffin, being lined with lead, sank. Fortunately there had been no loss of life, for no one had been struck by the falling coffin, and the widower together with the other persons in the boat had been rescued, though not without difficulty.

What had caused the accident? One story, said the reporter, was that a lunatic had jumped overboard, and in his fall had wrenched the coffin from its lashings. Perhaps the story of the falling body had been invented to cover up the remissness of those responsible for lowering the coffin, who had used tackle that was too weak, so that the lead-weighted box had broken away of itself. Anyhow, the officers were extremely reticent.

In another part of the paper was a brief notice to the effect that the body of an unknown man, apparently about thirty-five years of age, had been picked up in Naples harbour. There was a bullet-wound in the head. No one connected this with the accident which occurred when the coffin was being lowered.

Before my own eyes, however, as I read the brief paragraphs, there loomed from the printed page the ghostly countenance of the unhappy man whose story I have here set down.

LETTER FROM
AN UNKNOWN WOMAN

R., THE famous novelist, had been away on a brief holiday in the mountains. Reaching Vienna early in the morning, he bought a newspaper at the station, and when he glanced at the date was reminded that it was his birthday. "Forty-one!"—the thought came like a flash. He was neither glad nor sorry at the realization. He hailed a taxi, and skimmed the newspaper as he drove home. His man reported that there had been a few callers during the master's absence, besides some telephone messages. A bundle of letters was awaiting him. Looking indifferently at these, he opened one or two because he was interested in the senders, but laid aside for the time a bulky packet addressed in a strange handwriting. At ease in an armchair, he drank his morning tea, finished the newspaper, and read a few circulars. Then, having lighted a cigar, he turned to the remaining letter.

It was a manuscript rather than an ordinary letter, comprising several dozen hastily penned sheets in a feminine handwriting. Involuntarily he examined the envelope once more, in case he might have overlooked a covering letter. But there was nothing of the kind, no signature, and no sender's address on either envelope or contents. "Strange," he thought, as he began to read the manuscript. The first words were a superscription: "To you, who have never known me." He was perplexed. Was this addressed to him, or to some imaginary being? His curiosity suddenly awakened, he read as follows:

My boy died yesterday. For three days and three nights
I have been wrestling with Death for this frail little life.
During forty consecutive hours, while the fever of influenza was shaking his poor burning body, I sat beside
his bed. I put cold compresses on his forehead; day and
night, night and day. I held his restless little hands. The
third evening, my strength gave out. My eyes closed without my being aware of it, and for three or four hours I
must have slept on the hard stool. Meanwhile, Death
took him. There he lies, my darling boy, in his narrow
cot, just as he died. Only his eyes have been closed, his
wise, dark eyes; and his hands have been crossed over his
breast. Four candles are burning, one at each corner of
the bed. I cannot bear to look, I cannot bear to move; for
when the candles flicker, shadows chase one another over
his face and his closed lips. It looks as if his features
stirred, and I could almost fancy that he is not dead after
all, that he will wake, and with his clear voice will say
something childishly loving. But I know that he is dead;
and I will not look again, to hope once more, and once
more to be disappointed. I know, I know, my boy died
yesterday. Now I have only you left in the world; only
you, who do not know me; you, who are enjoying yourself all unheeding, sporting with men and things. Only
you, who have never known me, and whom I have never
ceased to love.

I have lighted a fifth candle, and am sitting at the table
writing to you. I cannot stay alone with my dead child
without pouring my heart out to some one; and to whom
should I do that in this dreadful hour if not to you, who
have been and still are all in all to me? Perhaps I shall
not be able to make myself plain to you. Perhaps you
will not be able to understand me. My head feels so

heavy; my temples are throbbing; my limbs are aching. I think I must be feverish. Influenza is raging in this quarter, and probably I have caught the infection. I should not be sorry if I could join my child in that way, instead of making short work of myself. Sometimes it seems dark before my eyes, and perhaps I shall not be able to finish this letter; but I shall try with all my strength, this one and only time, to speak to you, my beloved, to you who have never known me.

To you only do I want to speak, that I may tell you everything for the first time. I should like you to know the whole of my life, of that life which has always been yours, and of which you have known nothing. But you shall only know my secret after I am dead, when there will be no one whom you will have to answer; you shall only know it if that which is now shaking my limbs with cold and with heat should really prove, for me, the end. If I have to go on living, I shall tear up this letter and shall keep the silence I have always kept. If you ever hold it in your hands, you may know that a dead woman is telling you her life story; the story of a life which was yours from its first to its last fully conscious hour. You need have no fear of my words. A dead woman wants nothing; neither love, nor compassion, nor consolation. I have only one thing to ask of you, that you believe to the full what the pain in me forces me to disclose to you. Believe my words, for I ask nothing more of you; a mother will not speak falsely beside the death-bed of her only child.

I am going to tell you my whole life, the life which did not really begin until the day I first saw you. What I can recall before that day is gloomy and confused, a memory as of a cellar filled with dusty, dull, and cobwebbed

things and people—a place with which my heart has no
concern. When you came into my life, I was thirteen, and
I lived in the house where you live today, in the very
house in which you are reading this letter, the last breath
of my life. I lived on the same floor, for the door of our
flat was just opposite the door of yours. You will certainly have forgotten us. You will long ago have forgotten the accountant's widow in her threadbare mourning,
and the thin, half-grown girl. We were always so quiet;
characteristic examples of shabby gentility. It is unlikely
that you ever heard our name, for we had no plate on
our front door, and no one ever came to see us. Besides,
it is so long ago, fifteen or sixteen years. Impossible that
you should remember. But I, how passionately I remember every detail. As if it had just happened, I recall the
day, the hour, when I first heard of you, first saw you.
How could it be otherwise, seeing that it was then the
world began for me? Have patience awhile, and let me
tell you everything from first to last. Do not grow weary
of listening to me for a brief space, since I have not been
weary of loving you my whole life long.

Before you came, the people who lived in your flat
were horrid folk, always quarrelling. Though they were
wretchedly poor themselves, they hated us for our poverty because we held aloof from them. The man was given
to drink, and used to beat his wife. We were often wak-
ened in the night by the clatter of falling chairs and
breaking plates. Once, when he had beaten her till the
blood came, she ran out on the landing with her hair
streaming, followed by her drunken husband abusing
her, until all the people came out on to the staircase and
threatened to send for the police. My mother would have
nothing to do with them. She forbade me to play with

the children, who took every opportunity of venting their spleen on me for this refusal. When they met me in the street, they would call me names; and once they threw a snowball at me which was so hard that it cut my forehead. Every one in the house detested them, and we all breathed more freely when something happened and they had to leave—I think the man had been arrested for theft. For a few days there was a "To Let" notice at the main door. Then it was taken down, and the caretaker told us that the flat had been rented by an author, who was a bachelor, and was sure to be quiet. That was the first time I heard your name.

A few days later, the flat was thoroughly cleaned, and the painters and decorators came. Of course they made a lot of noise, but my mother was glad, for she said that would be the end of the disorder next door. I did not see you during the move. The decorations and furnishings were supervised by your servant, the little grey-haired man with such a serious demeanour, who had obviously been used to service in good families. He managed everything in a most businesslike way, and impressed us all very much. A high-class domestic of this kind was something quite new in our suburban flats. Besides, he was extremely civil, but was never hail-fellow-well-met with the ordinary servants. From the outset he treated my mother respectfully, as a lady; and he was always courteous even to little me. When he had occasion to mention your name, he did so in a way which showed that his feeling towards you was that of a family retainer. I used to love good old John for this, though I envied him at the same time because it was his privilege to see you constantly and to serve you.

Do you know why I am telling you these trifles? I want

you to understand how it was that from the very beginning your personality came to exercise so much power
over me when I was still a shy and timid child. Before I
had actually seen you, there was a halo round your head.
You were enveloped in an atmosphere of wealth, marvel,
and mystery. People whose lives are narrow, are avid of
novelty; and in this little suburban house we were all
impatiently awaiting your arrival. In my own case, curiosity rose to fever point when I came home from school
one afternoon and found the furniture van in front of
the house. Most of the heavy things had gone up, and the
furniture movers were dealing with the smaller articles.
I stood at the door to watch and admire, for everything
belonging to you was so different from what I had been
used to. There were Indian idols, Italian sculptures, and
great, brightly coloured pictures. Last of all came books,
such lovely books, many more than I should have thought
possible. They were piled by the door. The manservant
stood there carefully dusting them one by one. I greedily
watched the pile as it grew. Your servant did not send me
away, but he did not encourage me either, so I was afraid
to touch any of them, though I should have so liked to
stroke the smooth leather bindings. I did glance timidly
at some of the titles; many of them were in French and
in English, and in languages of which I did not know a
single word. I should have liked to stand there watching
for hours, but my mother called me and I had to go in.

I thought about you the whole evening, although I
had not seen you yet. I had only about a dozen cheap
books, bound in worn cardboard. I loved them more than
anything else in the world, and was continually reading
and rereading them. Now I was wondering what the man
could be like who had such a lot of books, who had read

so much, who knew so many languages, who was rich
and at the same time so learned. The idea of so many
books aroused a kind of unearthly veneration. I tried to
picture you in my mind. You must be an old man with
spectacles and a long, white beard, like our geography
master, but much kinder, nicer-looking, and gentler. I
don't know why I was sure that you must be handsome,
for I fancied you to be an elderly man. That very night,
I dreamed of you for the first time.

Next day you moved in; but though I was on the watch
I could not get a glimpse of your face, and my failure in-
flamed my curiosity. At length I saw you, on the third
day. How astounded I was to find that you were quite
different from the ancient godfather conjured up by my
childish imagination. A bespectacled, good-natured old
fellow was what I had anticipated; and you came, looking
just as you still look, for you are one on whom the years
leave little mark. You were wearing a beautiful suit of
light-brown tweeds, and you ran upstairs two steps at a
time with the boyish ease that always characterizes your
movements. You were hat in hand, so that, with indescribable amazement, I could see your bright and lively
face and your youthful hair. Your handsome, slim, and
spruce figure was a positive shock to me. How strange it
was that in this first moment I should have plainly realized that which I and all others are continually surprised
at in you. I realized that you are two people rolled into
one: that you are an ardent, light-hearted youth, devoted
to sport and adventure; and at the same time, in your
art, a deeply read and highly cultured man, grave, and
with a keen sense of responsibility. Unconsciously I perceived what every one who knew you came to perceive,
that you led two lives. One of these was known to all, it

was the life open to the whole world; the other was
turned away from the world, and was fully known only to
yourself. I, a girl of thirteen, coming under the spell of
your attraction, grasped this secret of your existence, this
profound cleavage of your two lives, at the first glance.

Can you understand, now, what a miracle, what an
alluring enigma, you must have seemed to me, the child?
Here was a man whom every one spoke of with respect
because he wrote books, and because he was famous in
the great world. Of a sudden he had revealed himself to
me as a boyish, cheerful young man of five-and-twenty!
I need hardly tell you that henceforward, in my restricted
world, you were the only thing that interested me; that
my life revolved round yours with the fidelity proper to
a girl of thirteen. I watched you, watched your habits,
watched the people who came to see you—and all this
increased instead of diminishing my interest in your personality, for the two-sidedness of your nature was reflected in the diversity of your visitors. Some of them
were young men, comrades of yours, carelessly dressed
students with whom you laughed and larked. Some of
them were ladies who came in motors. Once the conductor of the opera—the great man whom before this
I had seen only from a distance, baton in hand—called
on you. Some of them were girls, young girls still attend-
ing the commercial school, who shyly glided in at the
door. A great many of your visitors were women. I
thought nothing of this, not even when, one morning, as
I was on my way to school, I saw a closely veiled lady
coming away from your flat. I was only just thirteen, and
in my immaturity I did not in the least realize that the
eager curiosity with which I scanned all your doings was
already love.

But I know the very day and hour when I consciously gave my whole heart to you. I had been for a walk with a schoolfellow, and we were standing at the door chattering. A motor drove up. You jumped out, in the impatient, springy fashion which has never ceased to charm me, and were about to go in. An impulse made me open the door for you, and this brought me in your path, so that we almost collided. You looked at me with a cordial, gracious, all-embracing glance, which was almost a caress. You smiled at me tenderly—yes, tenderly, is the word—and said gently, nay, confidentially: "Thanks so much."

That was all. But from this moment, from the time when you looked at me so gently, so tenderly, I was yours. Later, before long indeed, I was to learn that this was a way you had of looking at all women with whom you came in contact. It was a caressive and alluring glance, at once enfolding and disclothing, the glance of the born seducer. Involuntarily, you looked in this way at every shopgirl who served you, at every maidservant who opened the door to you. It was not that you consciously longed to possess all these women, but your impulse towards the sex unconsciously made your eyes melting and warm whenever they rested on a woman. At thirteen, I had no thought of this; and I felt as if I had been bathed in fire. I believed that the tenderness was for me, for me only; and in this one instant the woman was awakened in the half-grown girl, the woman who was to be yours for all future time.

"Who was that?" asked my friend. At first, I could not answer. I found it impossible to utter your name. It had suddenly become sacred to me, had become my secret. "Oh, it's just some one who lives in the house," I said awkwardly. "Then why did you blush so fiery red when he looked at you?" inquired my schoolfellow with the malice of an inquisitive child. I felt that she was making fun of me, and was reaching out towards my secret, and this coloured my cheeks more than ever. I was deliberately rude to her: "You silly idiot," I said angrily —I should have liked to throttle her. She laughed mockingly, until the tears came into my eyes from impotent rage. I left her at the door and ran upstairs.

I have loved you ever since. I know full well that you are used to hearing women say that they love you. But I am sure that no one else has ever loved you so slavishly, with such doglike fidelity, with such devotion, as I did and do. Nothing can equal the unnoticed love of a child. It is hopeless and subservient; it is patient and passionate; it is something which the covetous love of a grown woman, the love that is unconsciously exacting, can never be. None but lonely children can cherish such a passion. The others will squander their feelings in companionship, will dissipate them in confidential talks. They have heard and read much of love, and they know that it comes to all. They play with it like a toy; they flaunt it as a boy flaunts his first cigarette. But I had no confidant; I had been neither taught nor warned; I was inexperienced and unsuspecting. I rushed to meet my fate. Everything that stirred in me, all that happened to me, seemed to be centred upon you, upon my imaginings of you. My father had died long before. My mother could think of nothing but her troubles, of the difficulties of making ends meet upon her narrow pension, so that she had little in common with a growing girl. My schoolfellows, half-enlightened and half-corrupted, were uncongenial to me because of their frivolous outlook upon that which to me was a supreme passion. The upshot was that everything which surged up in me, all which in other girls of my age is usually scattered, was focused upon you. You became for me—what simile can do justice to my feelings? You became for me the whole of my life. Nothing existed for me except in so far as it related to you. Nothing had meaning for me unless it bore upon you in some way. You had changed everything for me. Hitherto I had been indifferent at school, and undistinguished. Now, of a sudden, I was the first. I read book upon book, far into the night, for I knew that you were a book-lover. To my mother's astonishment, I began, almost stubbornly, to practise the piano, for I fancied that you were fond of music. I stitched and mended my clothes, to make them neat for your eyes. It was a torment to me that there was a square patch in my old school-apron (cut down from one of my mother's overalls). I was afraid you might notice it and would despise me, so I used to cover the patch with my satchel when I was on the staircase. I was terrified lest you should catch sight of it. What a fool I was! You hardly ever looked at me again.

Yet my days were spent in waiting for you and watching you. There was a judas in our front door, and through this a glimpse of your door could be had. Don't laugh at me, dear. Even now, I am not ashamed of the hours I spent at this spy-hole. The hall was icy cold, and I was afraid of exciting my mother's suspicions. But there I would watch through the long afternoons, during those months and years, book in hand, tense as a violin string, and vibrating at the touch of your nearness. I was ever near you, and ever tense; but you were no more aware of it than you were aware of the tension of the mainspring of the watch in your pocket, faithfully recording the hours for you, accompanying your footsteps with its unheard ticking and vouchsafed only a hasty glance for one second among millions. I knew all about you, your habits, the neckties you wore; I knew each one of your suits. Soon I was familiar with your regular visitors, and had my likes and dislikes among them. From my thirteenth to my sixteenth year, my every hour was yours. What follies did I not commit? I kissed the door-handle you had touched; I picked up a cigarette end you had thrown away, and it was sacred to me because your lips had pressed it. A hundred times, in the evening, on one pretext or another, I ran out into the street in order to see in which room your light was burning, that I might be more fully conscious of your invisible presence. During the weeks when you were away (my heart always seemed to stop beating when I saw John carry your portmanteau downstairs), life was devoid of meaning. Out of sorts, bored to death, and in an ill-humour, I wandered about not knowing what to do, and had to take precautions lest my tear-dimmed eyes should betray my despair to my mother.

I know that what I am writing here is a record of grotesque absurdities, of a girl's extravagant fantasies. I ought to be ashamed of them; but I am not ashamed, for never was my love purer and more passionate than at this time. I could spend hours, days, in telling you how I lived with you though you hardly knew me by sight. Of course you hardly knew me, for if I met you on the stairs and could not avoid the encounter, I would hasten by with lowered head, afraid of your burning glance, hasten like one who is jumping into the water to avoid being singed. For hours, days, I could tell you of those years you have long since forgotten; could unroll all the calendar of your life: but I will not weary you with details.

Only one more thing I should like to tell you dating from this time, the most splendid experience of my childhood. You must not laugh at it, for, trifle though you may deem it, to me it was of infinite significance.

It must have been a Sunday. You were away, and your man was dragging back the heavy rugs, which he had been beating, through the open door of the flat. They were rather too much for his strength, and I summoned up courage to ask whether he would let me help him. He was surprised, but did not refuse. Can I ever make you understand the awe, the pious veneration, with which I set foot in your dwelling, with which I saw your world—the writing-table at which you were accustomed to sit (there were some flowers on it in a blue crystal vase), the pictures, the books? I had no more than a stolen glance, though the good John would no doubt have let me see more had I ventured to ask him. But it was enough for me to absorb the atmosphere, and to provide fresh nourishment for my endless dreams of you in waking and sleeping.

This swift minute was the happiest of my childhood. I wanted to tell you of it, so that you who do not know me might at length begin to understand how my life hung upon yours. I wanted to tell you of that minute, and also of the dreadful hour which so soon followed. As I have explained, my thoughts of you had made me oblivious to all else. I paid no attention to my mother's doings, or to those of any of our visitors. I failed to notice that an elderly gentleman, an Innsbruck merchant, a distant family connexion of my mother, came often and stayed for a long time. I was glad that he took Mother to the theatre sometimes, for this left me alone, undisturbed in my thoughts of you, undisturbed in the watch-

ing which was my chief, my only pleasure. But one day
my mother summoned me with a certain formality, saying that she had something serious to talk to me about.
I turned pale, and felt my heart throb. Did she suspect
anything? Had I betrayed myself in some way? My first
thought was of you, of my secret, of that which linked
me with life. But my mother was herself embarrassed. It
had never been her way to kiss me. Now she kissed me
affectionately more than once, drew me to her on the
sofa, and began hesitatingly and rather shamefacedly to
tell me that her relative, who was a widower, had made
her a proposal of marriage, and that, mainly for my sake,
she had decided to accept. I palpitated with anxiety, having only one thought, that of you. "We shall stay here,
shan't we?" I stammered out. "No, we are going to Innsbruck, where Ferdinand has a fine villa." I heard no
more. Everything seemed to turn black before my eyes. I
learned afterwards that I had fainted. I clasped my hands
convulsively, and fell like a lump of lead. I cannot tell
you all that happened in the next few days; how I, a
powerless child, vainly revolted against the mighty elders.
Even now, as I think of it, my hand shakes so that I can
scarcely write. I could not disclose the real secret, and
therefore my opposition seemed ill-tempered obstinacy.
No one told me anything more. All the arrangements
were made behind my back. The hours when I was at
school were turned to account. Each time I came home
some new article had been removed or sold. My life
seemed falling to pieces; and at last one day, when I returned to dinner, the furniture movers had cleared the
flat. In the empty rooms there were some packed trunks,
and two camp-beds for Mother and myself. We were to

sleep there one night more, and were then to go to Innsbruck.

On this last day I suddenly made up my mind that I
could not live without being near you. You were all the
world to me. It is difficult to say what I was thinking of,
and whether in this hour of despair I was able to think
at all. My mother was out of the house. I stood up, just as
I was, in my school dress, and went over to your door. Yet
I can hardly say that I went. With stiff limbs and trembling joints, I seemed to be drawn towards your door as
by a magnet. It was in my mind to throw myself at your
feet, and to beg you to keep me as a maid, as a slave. I
cannot help feeling afraid that you will laugh at this
infatuation of a girl of fifteen. But you would not laugh
if you could realize how I stood there on the chilly landing, rigid with apprehension, and yet drawn onward by
an irresistible force; how my arm seemed to lift itself in
spite of me. The struggle appeared to last for endless, terrible seconds; and then I rang the bell. The shrill noise
still sounds in my ears. It was followed by a silence in
which my heart wellnigh stopped beating, and my blood
stagnated, while I listened for your coming.

But you did not come. No one came. You must have
been out that afternoon, and John must have been away
too. With the dead note of the bell still sounding in my
ears, I stole back into our empty dwelling, and threw
myself exhausted upon a rug, tired out by these few paces
as if I had been wading through deep snow for hours. Yet
beneath this exhaustion there still glowed the determination to see you, to speak to you, before they carried
me away. I can assure you that there were no sensual
longings in my mind; I was still ignorant, just because I

never thought of anything but you. All I wanted was to see you once more, to cling to you. Throughout that dreadful night I waited for you. Directly my mother had gone to sleep, I crept into the hall to listen for your return. It was a bitterly cold night in January. I was tired, my limbs ached, and there was no longer a chair on which I could sit; so I lay upon the floor, scourged by the draught that came under the door. In my thin dress I lay there, without any covering. I did not want to be warm, lest I should fall asleep and miss your footstep. Cramps seized me, so cold was it in the horrible darkness; again and again I had to stand up. But I waited, waited, waited for you, as for my fate.

At length (it must have been two or three in the morning) I heard the housedoor open, and footsteps on the stair. The sense of cold vanished, and a rush of heat passed over me. I softly opened the door, meaning to run out, to throw myself at your feet. . . . I cannot tell what I should have done in my frenzy. The steps drew nearer. A candle flickered. Tremblingly I held the doorhandle. Was it you coming up the stairs?

Yes, it was you, beloved; but you were not alone. I heard a gentle laugh, the rustle of silk, and your voice, speaking in low tones. There was a woman with you. . . .

I cannot tell how I lived through the rest of the night. At eight next morning, they took me with them to Innsbruck. I had no strength left to resist.

My boy died last night. I shall be alone once more, if I really have to go on living. Tomorrow, strange men will come, black-clad and uncouth, bringing with them a coffin for the body of my only child. Perhaps friends will

come as well, with wreaths—but what is the use of flowers on a coffin? They will offer consolation in one phrase
or another. Words, words, words! What can words help?
All I know is that I shall be alone again. There is nothing more terrible than to be alone among human beings.
That is what I came to realize during those interminable
two years in Innsbruck, from my sixteenth to my eight-
eenth year, when I lived with my people as a prisoner and
an outcast. My stepfather, a quiet, taciturn man, was
kind to me. My mother, as if eager to atone for an unwitting injustice, seemed ready to meet all my wishes.
Those of my own age would have been glad to befriend
me. But I repelled their advances with angry defiance. I
did not wish to be happy, I did not wish to live content
away from you; so I buried myself in a gloomy world of
self-torment and solitude. I would not wear the new and
gay dresses they bought for me. I refused to go to concerts or to the theatre, and I would not take part in cheerful excursions. I rarely left the house. Can you believe
me when I tell you that I hardly got to know a dozen
streets in this little town where I lived for two years?
Mourning was my joy; I renounced society and every
pleasure, and was intoxicated with delight at the morti-
fications I thus superadded to the lack of seeing you.
Moreover, I would let nothing divert me from my passionate longing to live only for you. Sitting alone at
home, hour after hour and day after day, I did nothing
but think of you, turning over in my mind unceasingly
my hundred petty memories of you, renewing every
movement and every time of waiting, rehearsing these
episodes in the theatre of my mind. The countless repeti-
tions of the years of my childhood from the day in which

you came into my life have so branded the details on my memory that I can recall every minute of those long-passed years as if they were yesterday.

Thus my life was still entirely centred in you. I bought all your books. If your name was mentioned in the newspaper, the day was a red-letter day. Will you believe me when I tell you that I have read your books so often that I know them by heart? Were any one to wake me in the night and quote a detached sentence, I could continue the passage unfalteringly even today, after thirteen years. Your every word was Holy Writ to me. The world existed for me only in relationship to you. In the Viennese newspapers I read the reports of concerts and first nights, wondering which would interest you most. When evening came, I accompanied you in imagination, saying to myself: "Now he is entering the hall; now he is taking his seat." Such were my fancies a thousand times, simply because I had once seen you at a concert.

Why should I recount these things? Why recount the tragic hopelessness of a forsaken child? Why tell it to you, who have never dreamed of my admiration or of my sorrow? But was I still a child? I was seventeen; I was eighteen; young fellows would turn to look after me in the street, but they only made me angry. To love any one but you, even to play with the thought of loving any one but you, would have been so utterly impossible to me, that the mere tender of affection on the part of another man seemed to me a crime. My passion for you remained just as intense, but it changed in character as my body grew and my senses awakened, becoming more ardent, more physical, more unmistakably the love of a grown woman. What had been hidden from the thoughts of the uninstructed child, of the girl who had rung your

door bell, was now my only longing. I wanted to give myself to you.

My associates believed me to be shy and timid. But I
had an absolute fixity of purpose. My whole being was
directed towards one end—back to Vienna, back to you.
I fought successfully to get my own way, unreasonable,
incomprehensible though it seemed to others. My stepfather was well-to-do, and looked upon me as his daughter. I insisted, however, that I would earn my own living, and at length got him to agree to my returning to
Vienna as employee in a dressmaking establishment belonging to a relative of his.

Need I tell you whither my steps first led me that
foggy autumn evening when, at last, at last, I found myself back in Vienna? I left my trunk in the cloakroom,
and hurried to a tram. How slowly it moved! Every stop
was a renewed vexation to me. In the end, I reached the
house. My heart leapt when I saw a light in your window.
The town, which had seemed so alien, so dreary, grew
suddenly alive for me. I myself lived once more, now that
I was near you, you who were my unending dream.
When nothing but the thin, shining pane of glass was
between you and my uplifted eyes, I could ignore the
fact that in reality I was as far from your mind as if I
had been separated by mountains and valleys and rivers.
Enough that I could go on looking at your window.
There was a light in it; that was your dwelling; you were
there; that was my world. For two years I had dreamed
of this hour, and now it had come. Throughout that
warm and cloudy evening I stood in front of your windows, until the light was extinguished. Not until then
did I seek my own quarters.

Evening after evening I returned to the same spot. Up

to six o'clock I was at work. The work was hard, and yet
I liked it, for the turmoil of the show-room masked the
turmoil in my heart. The instant the shutters were rolled
down, I flew to the beloved spot. To see you once more,
to meet you just once, was all I wanted; simply from a
distance to devour your face with my eyes. At length,
after a week, I did meet you, and then the meeting took
me by surprise. I was watching your window, when you
came across the street. In an instant, I was a child once
more, the girl of thirteen. My cheeks flushed. Although I
was longing to meet your eyes, I hung my head and hurried past you as if some one had been in pursuit. Afterwards I was ashamed of having fled like a schoolgirl, for
now I knew what I really wanted. I wanted to meet you;
I wanted you to recognize me after all these weary years,
to notice me, to love me.

For a long time you failed to notice me, although I
took up my post outside your house every night, even
when it was snowing, or when the keen wind of the
Viennese winter was blowing. Sometimes I waited for
hours in vain. Often, in the end, you would leave the
house in the company of friends. Twice I saw you with
a woman, and the fact that I was now awakened, that
there was something new and different in my feeling
towards you, was disclosed by the sudden heart-pang
when I saw a strange woman walking confidently with
you arm-in-arm. It was no surprise to me, for I had
known since childhood how many such visitors came to
your house; but now the sight aroused in me a definite
bodily pain. I had a mingled feeling of enmity and desire
when I witnessed this open manifestation of fleshly intimacy with another woman. For a day, animated by the
youthful pride from which, perhaps, I am not yet free,

I abstained from my usual visit; but how horrible was this empty evening of defiance and renunciation! The next night I was standing, as usual, in all humility, in front of your window; waiting, as I have ever waited, in front of your closed life.

At length came the hour when you noticed me. I marked your coming from a distance, and collected all my forces to prevent myself shrinking out of your path. As chance would have it, a loaded dray filled the street, so that you had to pass quite close to me. Involuntarily your eyes encountered my figure, and immediately, though you had hardly noticed the attentiveness in my gaze, there came into your face that expression with which you were wont to look at women. The memory of it darted through me like an electric shock—that caressive and alluring glance, at once enfolding and disclothing, with which, years before, you had awakened the girl to become the woman and the lover. For a moment or two your eyes thus rested on me, for a space during which I could not turn my own eyes away, and then you had passed. My heart was beating so furiously that I had to slacken my pace; and when, moved by irresistible curiosity, I turned to look back, I saw that you were standing and watching me. The inquisitive interest of your expression convinced me that you had not recognized me. You did not recognize me, either then or later. How can I describe my disappointment? This was the first of such disappointments: the first time I had to endure what has always been my fate; that you have never recognized me. I must die, unrecognized. Ah, how can I make you understand my disappointment? During the years at Innsbruck I had never ceased to think of you. Our next meeting in Vienna was always in my thoughts. My fancies

varied with my mood, ranging from the wildest possibilities to the most delightful. Every conceivable varia-
tion had passed through my mind. In gloomy moments
it had seemed to me that you would repulse me, would
despise me, for being of no account, for being plain, or
importunate. I had had a vision of every possible form of
disfavour, coldness, or indifference. But never, in the
extremity of depression, in the utmost realization of my
own insignificance, had I conceived this most abhorrent
of possibilities—that you had never become aware of my
existence. I understand now (you have taught me!) that a
girl's or a woman's face must be for a man something
extraordinarily mutable. It is usually nothing more than
the reflexion of moods which pass as swiftly as an image
vanishes from a mirror. A man can readily forget a
woman's face, because age modifies its lights and shades,
and because at different times the dress gives it so different a setting. Resignation comes to a woman as her
knowledge grows. But I, who was still a girl, was unable
to understand your forgetfulness. My whole mind had
been full of you ever since I had first known you, and
this had produced in me the illusion that you must have
often thought of me and waited for me. How could I
have borne to go on living had I realized that I was nothing to you, that I had no place in your memory? Your
glance that evening, showing me as it did that on your
side there was not even a gossamer thread connecting
your life with mine, meant for me a first plunge into
reality, conveyed to me the first intimation of my destiny.

You did not recognize me. Two days later, when our
paths again crossed, and you looked at me with an approach to intimacy, it was not in recognition of the girl
who had loved you so long and whom you had awakened

to womanhood; it was simply that you knew the face of
the pretty lass of eighteen whom you had encountered at
the same spot two evenings before. Your expression was
one of friendly surprise, and a smile fluttered about your
lips. You passed me as before, and as before you promptly
slackened your pace. I trembled, I exulted, I longed for
you to speak to me. I felt that for the first time I had
become alive for you; I, too, walked slowly, and did not
attempt to evade you. Suddenly, I heard your step behind me. Without turning round, I knew that I was
about to hear your beloved voice directly addressing me.
I was almost paralysed by the expectation, and my heart
beat so violently that I thought I should have to stand
still. You were at my side. You greeted me cordially, as
if we were old acquaintances—though you did not really
know me, though you have never known anything about
my life. So simple and charming was your manner that I
was able to answer you without hesitation. We walked
along the street, and you asked me whether we could
not have supper together. I agreed. What was there I
could have refused you?

We supped in a little restaurant. You will not remember where it was. To you it will be one of many such.
For what was I? One among hundreds; one adventure,
one link in an endless chain. What happened that evening to keep me in your memory? I said very little, for I
was so intensely happy to have you near me and to hear
you speak to me. I did not wish to waste a moment upon
questions or foolish words. I shall never cease to be thankful to you for that hour, for the way in which you justi-
fied my ardent admiration. I shall never forget the gentle
tact you displayed. There was no undue eagerness, no
hasty offer of a caress. Yet from the first moment you

displayed so much friendly confidence that you would
have won me even if my whole being had not long ere
this been yours. Can I make you understand how much
it meant to me that my five years of expectation were so
perfectly fulfilled?

The hour grew late, and we came away from the restaurant. At the door you asked me whether I was in any
hurry, or still had time to spare. How could I hide from
you that I was yours? I said I had plenty of time. With a
momentary hesitation, you asked me whether I would
not come to your rooms for a talk. "I shall be delighted,"
I answered with alacrity, thus giving frank expression to
my feelings. I could not fail to notice that my ready assent surprised you. I am not sure whether your feeling
was one of vexation or pleasure, but it was obvious to me
that you were surprised. Today, of course, I understand
your astonishment. I know now that it is usual for a
woman, even though she may ardently desire to give herself to a man, to feign reluctance, to simulate alarm or
indignation. She must be brought to consent by urgent
pleading, by lies, adjurations, and promises. I know that
only professional prostitutes are accustomed to answer
such an invitation with a perfectly frank assent—prostitutes, or simple-minded, immature girls. How could you
know that, in my case, the frank assent was but the voic-
ing of an eternity of desire, the uprush of yearnings that
had endured for a thousand days and more?

In any case, my manner aroused your attention; I had
become interesting to you. As we were walking along together, I felt that during our conversation you were trying to sample me in some way. Your perceptions, your
assured touch in the whole gamut of human emotions,
made you realize instantly that there was something un-

usual here; that this pretty, complaisant girl carried a secret about with her. Your curiosity had been awakened, and your discreet questions showed that you were trying to pluck the heart out of my mystery. But my replies were evasive. I would rather seem a fool than disclose my secret to you.

We went up to your flat. Forgive me, beloved, for saying that you cannot possibly understand all that it meant to me to go up those stairs with you—how I was mad, tortured, almost suffocated with happiness. Even now I can hardly think of it without tears, but I have no tears left. Everything in that house had been steeped in my passion; everything was a symbol of my childhood and its longing. There was the door behind which a thousand times I had awaited your coming; the stairs on which I had heard your footstep, and where I had first seen you; the judas through which I had watched your comings and goings; the door-mat on which I had once knelt; the sound of a key in the lock, which had always been a signal to me. My childhood and its passions were nested within these few yards of space. Here was my whole life, and it surged around me like a great storm, for all was being fulfilled, and I was going with you, I with you, into your, into our, house. Think (the way I am phrasing it sounds trivial, but I know no better words) that up to your door was the world of reality, the dull everyday world which had been that of all my previous life. At this door began the magic world of my childish imaginings, Aladdin's realm. Think how, a thousand times, I had had my burning eyes fixed upon this door through which I was now passing, my head in a whirl, and you will have an inkling—no more—of all that this tremendous minute meant to me.

I stayed with you that night. You did not dream that before you no man had ever touched or seen my body. How could you fancy it, when I made no resistance, and when I suppressed every trace of shame, fearing lest I might betray the secret of my love? That would certainly have alarmed you; you care only for what comes and goes easily, for that which is light of touch, is imponderable. You dread being involved in any one else's destiny. You like to give yourself freely to all the world—but not to make any sacrifices. When I tell you that I gave myself to you as a maiden, do not misunderstand me. I am not making any charge against you. You did not entice me, deceive me, seduce me. I threw myself into your arms; went out to meet my fate. I have nothing but thankfulness towards you for the blessedness of that night. When I opened my eyes in the darkness and you were beside me, I felt that I must be in heaven, and I was amazed that the stars were not shining on me. Never, beloved, have I repented giving myself to you that night. When you were sleeping beside me, when I listened to your breathing, touched your body, and felt myself so near you, I shed tears for very happiness.

I went away early in the morning. I had to go to my work, and I wanted to leave before your servant came. When I was ready to go, you put your arm round me and looked at me for a very long time. Was some obscure memory stirring in your mind; or was it simply that my radiant happiness made me seem beautiful to you? You kissed me on the lips, and I moved to go. You asked me: "Would you not like to take a few flowers with you?" There were four white roses in the blue crystal vase on the writing-table (I knew it of old from that stolen glance of childhood), and you gave them to me. For days they were mine to kiss.

We had arranged to meet on a second evening. Again it was full of wonder and delight. You gave me a third night. Then you said that you were called away from Vienna for a time—oh, how I had always hated those journeys of yours!—and promised that I should hear from you as soon as you came back. I would only give you a poste-restante address, and did not tell you my real name. I guarded my secret. Once more you gave me roses at parting—at parting.

Day after day for two months I asked myself . . . No, I will not describe the anguish of my expectation and despair. I make no complaint. I love you just as you are, ardent and forgetful, generous and unfaithful. I love you just as you have always been. You were back long before the two months were up. The light in your windows showed me that, but you did not write to me. In my last hours I have not a line in your handwriting, not a line from you to whom my life was given. I waited, waited despairingly. You did not call me to you, did not write a word, not a word. . . .

My boy who died yesterday was yours too. He was your son, the child of one of those three nights. I was yours, and yours only from that time until the hour of his birth. I felt myself sanctified by your touch, and it would not have been possible for me then to accept any other man's caresses. He was our boy, dear; the child of my fully conscious love and of your careless, spendthrift, almost unwitting tenderness. Our child, our son, our only child. Perhaps you will be startled, perhaps merely surprised.

You will wonder why I never told you of this boy; and why, having kept silence throughout the long years, I only tell you of him now, when he lies in his last sleep, about to leave me for all time—never, never to return. How could I have told you? I was a stranger, a girl who had shown herself only too eager to spend those three nights with you. Never would you have believed that I, the nameless partner in a chance encounter, had been faithful to you, the unfaithful. You would never, without misgivings, have accepted the boy as your own. Even if, to all appearance, you had trusted my word, you would still have cherished the secret suspicion that I had seized an opportunity of fathering upon you, a man of means, the child of another lover. You would have been suspicious. There would always have been a shadow of mistrust between you and me. I could not have borne it. Besides, I know you. Perhaps I know you better than you know yourself. You love to be carefree, light of heart, perfectly at ease; and that is what you understand by love. It would have been repugnant to you to find yourself suddenly in the position of father; to be made responsible, all at once, for a child's destiny. The breath of freedom is the breath of life to you, and you would have felt me to be a tie. Inwardly, even in defiance of your conscious will, you would have hated me as an embodied claim. Perhaps only now and again, for an hour or for a fleeting minute, should I have seemed a burden to you, should I have been hated by you. But it was my pride that I should never be a trouble or a care to you all my life long. I would rather take the whole burden on myself than be a burden to you; I wanted to be the one among all the women you had intimately known of whom you would never think except with love and thankfulness. In actual fact, you never thought of me at all. You forgot me.

I am not accusing you. Believe me, I am not complaining. You must forgive me if for a moment, now and again, it seems as if my pen had been dipped in gall. You must forgive me; for my boy, our boy, lies dead there beneath the flickering candles. I have clenched my fists against God, and have called him a murderer, for I have been almost beside myself with grief. Forgive me for complaining. I know that you are kindhearted, and always ready to help. You will help the merest stranger at a word. But your kindliness is peculiar. It is unbounded. Any one may have of yours as much as he can grasp with both hands. And yet, I must own, your kindliness works sluggishly. You need to be asked. You help those who call for help; you help from shame, from weakness, and not from sheer joy in helping. Let me tell you openly that those who are in affliction and torment are not dearer to you than your brothers in happiness. Now, it is hard, very hard, to ask anything of such as you, even of the kindest among you. Once, when I was still a child, I watched through the judas in our door how you gave something to a beggar who had rung your bell. You gave quickly and freely, almost before he spoke. But there was a certain nervousness and haste in your manner, as if your chief concern were to be speedily rid of him; you seemed to be afraid to meet his eye. I have never forgotten this uneasy and timid way of giving help, this shunning of a word of thanks. That is why I never turned to you in my difficulty. Oh, I know that you would have given me all the help I needed, in spite of a doubt that my child was yours. You would have offered me comfort, and have given me money, an ample supply of money; but always with a masked impatience, a secret desire to shake off trouble. I even believe that you would have advised me to rid myself of the coming child. This was what I dreaded above all, for I knew that I should do whatever you wanted. But the child was all in all to me. It was yours; it was you reborn—not the happy and carefree you, whom I could never hope to keep; but you, given to me for my very own, flesh of my flesh, intimately intertwined with my own life. At length I held you fast; I could feel your life-blood flowing through my veins; I could nourish you, caress you, kiss you, as often as my soul yearned. That was why I was so happy when I knew that I was with child by you, and that is why I kept the secret from you. Henceforward you could not escape me; you were mine.

But you must not suppose that the months of waiting passed so happily as I had dreamed in my first transports. They were full of sorrow and care, full of loathing for the baseness of mankind. Things went hard with me. I could not stay at work during the later months, for my stepfather's relatives would have noticed my condition, and would have sent the news home. Nor would I ask my mother for money; so until my time came I managed to live by the sale of some trinkets. A week before my confinement, the few crown-pieces that remained to me were stolen by my laundress, so I had to go to the maternity hospital. The child, your son, was born there, in that asylum of wretchedness, among the very poor, the outcast, and the abandoned. It was a deadly place. Everything was strange, was alien. We were all alien to one another, as we lay there in our loneliness, filled with mutual hatred, thrust together only by our kinship of poverty and distress into this crowded ward, reeking of chloroform and blood, filled with cries and moaning. A patient in these wards loses all individuality, except such as remains in the name at the head of the clinical record. What lies in the bed is merely a piece of quivering flesh, an object of study. . . .

I ask your forgiveness for speaking of these things. I shall never speak of them again. For eleven years I have kept silence, and shall soon be dumb for evermore. Once, at least, I had to cry aloud, to let you know how dearly bought was this child, this boy who was my delight, and who now lies dead. I had forgotten those dreadful hours, forgotten them in his smiles and his voice, forgotten them in my happiness. Now, when he is dead, the torment has come to life again; and I had, this once, to give it utterance. But I do not accuse you; only God, only God who is the author of such purposeless affliction. Never have I cherished an angry thought of you. Not even in the utmost agony of giving birth did I feel any resentment against you; never did I repent the nights when I enjoyed your love; never did I cease to love you, or to bless the hour when you came into my life. Were it necessary for me, fully aware of what was coming, to relive that time in hell, I would do it gladly, not once, but many times.

Our boy died yesterday, and you never knew him. His bright little personality has never come into the most fugitive contact with you, and your eyes have never rested on him. For a long time after our son was born, I kept myself hidden from you. My longing for you had become less overpowering. Indeed, I believe I loved you less passionately. Certainly, my love for you did not hurt so much, now that I had the boy. I did not wish to divide

myself between you and him, and so I did not give myself
to you, who were happy and independent of me, but to
the boy who needed me, whom I had to nourish, whom I
could kiss and fondle. I seemed to have been healed of
my restless yearning for you. The doom seemed to have
been lifted from me by the birth of this other you, who
was truly my own. Rarely, now, did my feelings reach
out towards you in your dwelling. One thing only—on
your birthday I have always sent you a bunch of white
roses, like the roses you gave me after our first night of
love. Has it ever occurred to you, during these ten or
eleven years, to ask yourself who sent them? Have you
ever recalled having given such roses to a girl? I do not
know, and never shall know. For me it was enough to
send them to you out of the darkness; enough, once a
year, to revive my own memory of that hour.

You never knew our boy. I blame myself today for having hidden him from you, for you would have loved him.
You have never seen him smile when he first opened his
eyes after sleep, his dark eyes that were your eyes, the
eyes with which he looked merrily forth at me and the
world. He was so bright, so lovable. All your lightheartedness and your mobile imagination were his likewise—
in the form in which these qualities can show themselves
in a child. He would spend entranced hours playing with
things as you play with life; and then, grown serious,
would sit long over his books. He was you, reborn. The
mingling of sport and earnest, which is so characteristic
of you, was becoming plain in him; and the more he
resembled you, the more I loved him. He was good at his
lessons, so that he could chatter French like a magpie.
His exercise books were the tidiest in the class. And what
a fine, upstanding little man he was! When I took him to

the seaside in the summer, at Grado, women used to stop and stroke his fair hair. At Semmering, when he was tobogganing, people would turn round to gaze after him. He was so handsome, so gentle, so appealing. Last year, when he went to school as a boarder, he began to wear the collegiates' uniform of an eighteenth-century page, with a little dagger stuck in his belt—now he lies here in his shift, with pallid lips and crossed hands.

You will wonder how I could manage to give the boy so costly an upbringing, how it was possible for me to provide for him an entry into this bright and cheerful life of the well-to-do. Dear one, I am speaking to you from the darkness. Unashamed, I will tell you. Do not shrink from me. I sold myself. I did not become a street-walker, a common prostitute, but I sold myself. My friends, my lovers, were wealthy men. At first I sought them out, but soon they sought me, for I was (did you ever notice it?) a beautiful woman. Every one to whom I gave myself was devoted to me. They all became my grateful admirers. They all loved me—except you, except you whom I loved.

Will you despise me now that I have told you what I did? I am sure you will not. I know you will understand everything, will understand that what I did was done only for you, for your other self, for your boy. In the lying-in hospital I had tasted the full horror of poverty. I knew that, in the world of the poor, those who are down-trodden are always the victims. I could not bear to think that your son, your lovely boy, was to grow up in that abyss, amid the corruptions of the street, in the poisoned air of a slum. His delicate lips must not learn the speech of the gutter; his fine, white skin must not be chafed by the harsh and sordid underclothing of the

poor. Your son must have the best of everything, all the
wealth and all the lightheartedness of the world. He must
follow your footsteps through life, must dwell in the
sphere in which you had lived.

That is why I sold myself. It was no sacrifice to me, for
what are conventionally termed "honour" and "disgrace" were unmeaning words to me. You were the only
one to whom my body could belong, and you did not
love me, so what did it matter what I did with that body?
My companions' caresses, even their most ardent passion, never sounded my depths, although many of them
were persons I could not but respect, and although the
thought of my own fate made me sympathize with them
in their unrequited love. All these men were kind to me;
they all petted and spoiled me; they all paid me every
deference. One of them, a widower, an elderly man of
title, used his utmost influence until he secured your
boy's nomination to the school. This man loved me like
a daughter. Three or four times he urged me to marry
him. I could have been a countess today, mistress of a
lovely castle in Tyrol. I could have been free from care,
for the boy would have had a most affectionate father,
and I should have had a sedate, distinguished, and kindhearted husband. But I persisted in my refusal, though
I knew it gave him pain. It may have been foolish of me.
Had I yielded, I should have been living a safe and re-
tired life somewhere, and my child would still have been
with me. Why should I hide from you the reason for my
refusal? I did not want to bind myself. I wanted to remain free—for you. In my innermost self, in the unconscious, I continued to dream the dream of my childhood.
Some day, perhaps, you would call me to your side, were
it only for an hour. For the possibility of this one hour

I rejected everything else, simply that I might be free to answer your call. Since my first awakening to womanhood, what had my life been but waiting, a waiting upon your will?

In the end, the expected hour came. And still you never knew that it had come! When it came, you did not recognize me. You have never recognized me, never, never. I met you often enough, in theatres, at concerts, in the Prater, and elsewhere. Always my heart leapt, but always you passed me by, unheeding. In outward appearance I had become a different person. The timid girl was a woman now; beautiful, it was said; decked out in fine clothes; surrounded by admirers. How could you recognize in me one whom you had known as a shy girl in the subdued light of your bedroom? Sometimes my companion would greet you, and you would acknowledge the greeting as you glanced at me. But your look was always that of a courteous stranger, a look of deference, but not of recognition—distant, hopelessly distant. Once, I remember, this non-recognition, familiar as it had become, was a torture to me. I was in a box at the opera with a friend, and you were in the next box. The lights were lowered when the Overture began. I could no longer see your face, but I could feel your breathing quite close to me, just as when I was with you in your room; and on the velvet-covered partition between the boxes your slender hand was resting. I was filled with an infinite longing to bend down and kiss this hand, whose loving touch I had once known. Amid the turmoil of sound from the orchestra, the craving grew ever more intense. I had to hold myself in convulsively, to keep my lips away from your dear hand. At the end of the first act, I told my friend I wanted to leave. It was intolerable to me to have you sitting there beside me in the darkness, so near, and so estranged.

But the hour came once more, only once more. It was all but a year ago, on the day after your birthday. My thoughts had been dwelling on you more than ever, for I used to keep your birthday as a festival. Early in the morning I had gone to buy the white roses which I sent you every year in commemoration of an hour you had forgotten. In the afternoon I took my boy for a drive and we had tea together. In the evening we went to the theatre. I wanted him to look upon this day as a sort of mystical anniversary of his youth, though he could not know the reason. The next day I spent with my intimate of that epoch, a young and wealthy manufacturer of Brunn, with whom I had been living for two years. He was passionately fond of me, and he, too, wanted me to marry him. I refused, for no reason he could understand, although he loaded me and the child with presents, and was lovable enough in his rather stupid and slavish devotion. We went together to a concert, where we met a lively company. We all had supper at a restaurant in the Ringstrasse. Amid talk and laughter, I proposed that we should move on to a dancing hall. In general, such places, where the cheerfulness is always an expression of partial intoxication, are repulsive to me, and I would seldom go to them. But on this occasion some elemental force seemed at work in me, leading me to make the proposal, which was hailed with acclamation by the others. I was animated by an inexplicable longing, as if some extraordinary experience were awaiting me. As usual, every one was eager to accede to my whims. We went to the dancing hall, drank some champagne, and I had a sudden access of almost frenzied cheerfulness such as I had never

known. I drank one glass of wine after another, joined in
the chorus of a suggestive song, and was in a mood to
dance with glee. Then, all in a moment, I felt as if my
heart had been seized by an icy or a burning hand. You
were sitting with some friends at the next table, regarding me with an admiring and covetous glance, that glance
which had always thrilled me beyond expression. For the
first time in ten years you were looking at me again under the stress of all the unconscious passion in your nature. I trembled, and my hand shook so violently that
I nearly let my wine-glass fall. Fortunately my companions did not notice my condition, for their perceptions
were confused by the noise of laughter and music.

Your look became continually more ardent, and
touched my own senses to fire. I could not be sure
whether you had at last recognized me, or whether your
desires had been aroused by one whom you believed to be
a stranger. My cheeks were flushed, and I talked at ran-
dom. You could not help noticing the effect your glance
had on me. You made an inconspicuous movement of the
head, to suggest my coming into the ante-room for a moment. Then, having settled your bill, you took leave of
your associates and left the table, after giving me a further sign that you intended to wait for me outside. I
shook like one in the cold stage of a fever. I could no
longer answer when spoken to, could no longer control
the tumult of my blood. At this moment, as chance would
have it, a couple of Negroes with clattering heels began
a barbaric dance, to the accompaniment of their own
shrill cries. Every one turned to look at them, and I
seized my opportunity. Standing up, I told my friend
that I would be back in a moment, and followed you.

You were waiting for me in the lobby, and your face

lighted up when I came. With a smile on your lips, you
hastened to meet me. It was plain that you did not recognize me, neither the child, nor the girl of old days. Again,
to you, I was a new acquaintance. "Have you really got
an hour to spare for me?" you asked in a confident tone,
which showed that you took me for one of the women
whom any one can buy for a night. "Yes," I answered;
the same tremulous but perfectly acquiescent "Yes" that
you had heard from me in my girlhood, more than ten
years earlier, in the darkling street. "Tell me when we
can meet," you said. "Whenever you like," I replied, for
I knew nothing of shame where you were concerned. You
looked at me with a little surprise, with a surprise which
had in it the same flavour of doubt mingled with curiosity which you had shown before when you were astonished at the readiness of my acceptance. "Now?" you inquired, after a moment's hesitation. "Yes," I replied,
"let us go."

I was about to fetch my wrap from the cloak-room,
when I remembered that my Brunn friend had handed
in our things together, and that he had the ticket. It was
impossible to go back and ask him for it, and it seemed
to me even more impossible to renounce this hour with
you to which I had been looking forward for years. My
choice was instantly made. I gathered my shawl around
me, and went forth into the misty night, regardless not
only of my cloak, but regardless, likewise, of the kindhearted man with whom I had been living for years—
regardless of the fact that in this public way, before his
friends, I was putting him into the ludicrous position of
one whose mistress abandons him at the first nod of a
stranger. Inwardly, I was well aware how basely and un-
gratefully I was behaving towards a good friend. I knew

that my outrageous folly would alienate him from me
for ever, and that I was playing havoc with my life. But
what was his friendship, what was my own life, to me
when compared with the chance of again feeling your
lips on mine, of again listening to the tones of your voice.
Now that all is over and done with I can tell you this, can
let you know how I loved you. I believe that were you to
summon me from my death-bed, I should find strength
to rise in answer to your call.

There was a taxi at the door, and we drove to your
rooms. Once more I could listen to your voice, once more
I felt the ecstasy of being near you, and was almost as intoxicated with joy and confusion as I had been so long
before. I cannot describe it all to you, how what I had
felt ten years earlier was now renewed as we went up the
well-known stairs together; how I lived simultaneously
in the past and in the present, my whole being fused as
it were with yours. In your rooms, little was changed.
There were a few more pictures, a great many more
books, one or two additions to your furniture—but the
whole had the friendly look of an old acquaintance. On
the writing-table was the vase with the roses—my roses,
the ones I had sent you the day before as a memento of
the woman whom you did not remember, whom you did
not recognize, not even now when she was close to you,
when you were holding her hand and your lips were
pressed on hers. But it comforted me to see my flowers
there, to know that you had cherished something that
was an emanation from me, was the breath of my love for
you.

You took me in your arms. Again I stayed with you
for the whole of one glorious night. But even then you
did not recognize me. While I thrilled to your caresses,

it was plain to me that your passion knew no difference between a loving mistress and a meretrix, that your spendthrift affections were wholly concentrated in their own expression. To me, the stranger picked up at a dancing hall, you were at once affectionate and courteous. You would not treat me lightly, and yet you were full of an enthralling ardour. Dizzy with the old happiness, I was again aware of the two-sidedness of your nature, of that strange mingling of intellectual passion with sensual, which had already enslaved me to you in my childhood. In no other man have I ever known such complete surrender to the sweetness of the moment. No other has for the time being given himself so utterly as did you who, when the hour was past, were to relapse into an interminable and almost inhuman forgetfulness. But I, too, forgot myself. Who was I, lying in the darkness beside you? Was I the impassioned child of former days; was I the mother of your son; was I a stranger? Everything in this wonderful night was at one and the same time entrancingly familiar and entrancingly new. I prayed that the joy might last for ever.

But morning came. It was late when we rose, and you asked me to stay to breakfast. Over the tea, which an unseen hand had discreetly served in the dining-room, we talked quietly. As of old, you displayed a cordial frankness; and, as of old, there were no tactless questions, there was no curiosity about myself. You did not ask my name, nor where I lived. To you I was, as before, a casual adventure, a nameless woman, an ardent hour which leaves no trace when it is over. You told me that you were about to start on a long journey, that you were going to spend two or three months in northern Africa. The words broke in upon my happiness like a knell: "Past, past,

past and forgotten!" I longed to throw myself at your
feet, crying: "Take me with you, that you may at length
come to know me, at length after all these years!" But
I was timid, cowardly, slavish, weak. All I could say was:
"What a pity." You looked at me with a smile: "Are you
really sorry?"

For a moment I was as if frenzied. I stood up and
looked at you fixedly. Then I said: "The man I love has
always gone on a journey." I looked at you straight in
the eyes. "Now, now," I thought, "now he will recognize
me!" You only smiled, and said consolingly: "One comes
back after a time." I answered: "Yes, one comes back,
but one has forgotten by then."

I must have spoken with strong feeling, for my tone
moved you. You, too, rose, and looked at me wonderingly
and tenderly. You put your hands on my shoulders:
"Good things are not forgotten, and I shall not forget
you." Your eyes studied me attentively, as if you wished
to form an enduring image of me in your mind. When I
felt this penetrating glance, this exploration of my whole
being, I could not but fancy that the spell of your blind-
ness would at last be broken. "He will recognize me! He
will recognize me!" My soul trembled with expectation.

But you did not recognize me. No, you did not recognize me. Never had I been more of a stranger to you than
I was at that moment, for had it been otherwise you could
not possibly have done what you did a few minutes later.
You kissed me again, kissed me passionately. My hair
had been ruffled, and I had to tidy it once more. Standing
at the glass, I saw in it—and as I saw, I was overcome with
shame and horror—that you were surreptitiously slipping a couple of banknotes into my muff. I could hardly
refrain from crying out; I could hardly refrain from slap-

ping your face. You were paying me for the night I had
spent with you, me who had loved you since childhood,
me the mother of your son. To you I was only a prostitute
picked up at a dancing hall. It was not enough that you
should forget me; you had to pay me, and to debase me
by doing so.

I hastily gathered up my belongings, that I might escape as quickly as possible; the pain was too great. I
looked round for my hat. There it was, on the writing-
table, beside the vase with the white roses, my roses. I had
an irresistible desire to make a last effort to awaken your
memory. "Will you give me one of your white roses?"
"Of course," you answered, lifting them all out of the
vase. "But perhaps they were given you by a woman, a
woman who loves you?" "Maybe," you replied, "I don't
know. They were a present, but I don't know who sent
them; that's why I'm so fond of them." I looked at you
intently: "Perhaps they were sent you by a woman whom
you have forgotten!"

You were surprised. I looked at you yet more intently.
"Recognize me, only recognize me at last!" was the clam-
our of my eyes. But your smile, though cordial, had no
recognition in it. You kissed me yet again, but you did
not recognize me.

I hurried away, for my eyes were filling with tears, and
I did not want you to see. In the entry, as I precipitated
myself from the room, I almost cannoned into John, your
servant. Embarrassed but zealous, he got out of my way,
and opened the front door for me. Then, in this fugitive
instant, as I looked at him through my tears, a light suddenly flooded the old man's face. In this fugitive instant,
I tell you, he recognized me, the man who had never
seen me since my childhood. I was so grateful, that I

could have kneeled before him and kissed his hands.
I tore from my muff the banknotes with which you had
scourged me, and thrust them upon him. He glanced at
me in alarm—for in this instant I think he understood
more of me than you have understood in your whole life.
Every one, every one, has been eager to spoil me; every
one has loaded me with kindness. But you, only you, forgot me. You, only you, never recognized me.

My boy, our boy, is dead. I have no one left to love;
no one in the world, except you. But what can you be to
me—you who have never, never recognized me, you who
stepped across me as you might step across a stream, you
who trod on me as you might tread on a stone, you who
went on your way unheeding, while you left me to wait
for all eternity? Once I fancied that I could hold you for
my own; that I held you, the elusive, in the child. But he
was your son! In the night, he cruelly slipped away from
me on a journey; he has forgotten me, and will never
return. I am alone once more, more utterly alone than
ever. I have nothing, nothing from you. No child, no
word, no line of writing, no place in your memory. If
any one were to mention my name in your presence, to
you it would be the name of a stranger. Shall I not be
glad to die, since I am dead to you? Glad to go away,
since you have gone away from me?
Beloved, I am not blaming you. I do not wish to in-
trude my sorrows into your joyful life. Do not fear that
I shall ever trouble you further. Bear with me for giving
way to the longing to cry out my heart to you this once, in
the bitter hour when the boy lies dead. Only this once
I must talk to you. Then I shall slip back into obscurity,
and be dumb towards you as I have ever been. You will

not even hear my cry so long as I continue to live. Only when I am dead will this heritage come to you from one who has loved you more fondly than any other has loved you, from one whom you have never recognized, from one who has always been awaiting your summons and whom you have never summoned. Perhaps, perhaps, when you receive this legacy you will call to me; and for the first time I shall be unfaithful to you, for I shall not hear you in the sleep of death. Neither picture nor token do I leave you, just as you left me nothing, for never will you recognize me now. That was my fate in life, and it shall be my fate in death likewise. I shall not summon you in my last hour; I shall go my way leaving you ignorant of my name and my appearance. Death will be easy to me, for you will not feel it from afar. I could not die if my death were going to give you pain.

I cannot write any more. My head is so heavy; my limbs ache; I am feverish. I must lie down. Perhaps all will soon be over. Perhaps, this once, fate will be kind to me, and I shall not have to see them take away my boy. . . . I cannot write any more. Farewell, dear one, farewell. All my thanks go out to you. What happened was good, in spite of everything. I shall be thankful to you till my last breath. I am so glad that I have told you all. Now you will know, though you can never fully understand, how much I have loved you; and yet my love will never be a burden to you. It is my solace that I shall not fail you. Nothing will be changed in your bright and lovely life. Beloved, my death will not harm you. This comforts me.

But who, ah who, will now send you white roses on your birthday? The vase will be empty. No longer will come that breath, that aroma, from my life, which once

a year was breathed into your room. I have one last request—the first, and the last. Do it for my sake. Always
on your birthday—a day when one thinks of oneself—
get some roses and put them in the vase. Do it just as
others, once a year, have a Mass said for the beloved dead.
I no longer believe in God, and therefore I do not want
a Mass said for me. I believe in you alone. I love none
but you. Only in you do I wish to go on living—just one
day in the year, softly, quietly, as I have always lived near
you. Please do this, my darling, please do it. . . . My
first request, and my last. . . . Thanks, thanks. . . . I
love you, I love you. . . . Farewell. . . .

The letter fell from his nerveless hands. He thought
long and deeply. Yes, he had vague memories of a neighbour's child, of a girl, of a woman in a dancing hall—all
was dim and confused, like the flickering and shapeless
view of a stone in the bed of a swiftly running stream.
Shadows chased one another across his mind, but would
not fuse into a picture. There were stirrings of memory
in the realm of feeling, and still he could not remember.
It seemed to him that he must have dreamed of all these
figures, must have dreamed often and vividly—and yet
they had only been the phantoms of a dream. His eyes
wandered to the blue vase on the writing-table. It was
empty. For years it had not been empty on his birthday.
He shuddered, feeling as if an invisible door had been
suddenly opened, a door through which a chill breeze
from another world was blowing into his sheltered room.
An intimation of death came to him, and an intimation
of deathless love. Something welled up within him; and
the thought of the dead woman stirred in his mind, bodi-
less and passionate, like the sound of distant music.